Cover Art from National Gallery of Art
NGA.gov

Jacques Louis François Touzé French, 1747 – 1807
The Kiss Returned, in or before 1795 pen and black ink,
watercolor, and gouache overall: 19.7 x 14 cm (7 3/4 x 5 1/2 in.)
Samuel H. Kress Collection

It Started with a Kiss
A Pride and Prejudice Variation

Beth Wood

Chapter 1

Mr. Fitzwilliam Darcy shook his head, trying to force his dreams from his mind. He could not remember the last night he had not dreamt of Elizabeth. Even though she had rejected him quite soundly, he still loved her more than he thought possible. Her rejection of his suit made her more endearing. It was clear she would not allow a man's fortune to influence her decision in marriage. His dreams were becoming more and more realistic the closer he drew to Pemberley. He was now consumed with the image of Elizabeth, as his wife, coming out to greet him on his return home. He blushed, thinking of where his dreams led after a passionate welcoming embrace. Knowing it could never be, he determined it would be best to invent an excuse to ride ahead of the rest of his party. He needed to face his empty home on his own.

He finished dressing for the day then made his way to the door leading to his sister's room. The sun had not yet risen when he made his decision.

Tapping on Georgiana's door, Darcy prepared to tell a small fabrication. He hated any form of disguise, but did not want to concern his sister.

"What is it Fitzwilliam?" Georgiana asked after opening the door.

"I have found that I must ride ahead of our party," he replied. "When everyone awakes, would you mind explaining to them that I have had a letter from our steward and have decided to ride ahead? If I leave now I will be able to arrive at Pemberley today. I should then be able to receive everyone by the time you arrive on the morrow."

"Of course," Georgiana replied, a look of concern filling her eyes. "Is it anything serious?"

"Nothing you need to worry about," he replied.

Although Georgiana did not completely believe her brother's excuse, she did not want to question him too closely. She had watched him studiously avoiding Miss Bingley, and assumed he was trying to find a day of peace before the Bingleys became house guests at Pemberley.

As the first views of his ancestral home came into view, Darcy slipped from his horse, deciding to take a short rest. He sat on the grassy rise, closing his eyes for a moment. As soon as he envisioned showing this view to Elizabeth he wrestled his eyes open and continued on his way. *I must stop envisioning her in my life*, he reprimanded himself.

After handing the reigns of his horse to one of the grooms he turned toward the house. As he approached, he realized he must still have been dreaming. Elizabeth was walking toward him. Losing awareness of everything else, he reacted as he had in all of his dreams. He strode toward her with an unmistakable smile, whispering her name ever so slightly before pulling her into his arms and pressing his lips to her own.

To say that Elizabeth Bennet was surprised to find herself face to face with Mr. Darcy would be an understatement. She would not have agreed to visit his home if she had known he would be in residence. As she had convinced herself that he must now hate her for her rejection of his suit, her bewilderment increased at the look of absolute joy that radiated from his face. Her confusion became complete when he whispered her name and pulled her into a more passionate embrace than she had ever witnessed, let alone participated in. She was not sure why (and did not at that moment want to examine the reason), but she suddenly realized she was kissing him back with just as much abandon as he was kissing her.

As Darcy released her lips to kiss her neck and whisper endearments into her ear, Elizabeth's eyes opened slightly. The sight of her Aunt and Uncle Gardiner staring at them with looks filled with complete incredulity brought her back to her senses.

"Mr. Darcy," Elizabeth breathed out, stepping backward as a very red flush overtook her features.

The effect was immediate. He opened his eyes as his face lost all color.

"You called me Mr. Darcy," he said, with a very strained voice.

"I have always called you Mr. Darcy," she replied.

"But in my dreams, you always call me Fitzwilliam," he replied. If possible, even more color drained from his face. "Please tell me that I am dreaming."

"I would, but if I remember correctly, disguise of any sort is an abhorrence to you."

"What have I done?"

Taking encouragement from the fact he had just admitted that he dreamed of her, Elizabeth decided to try her best to lighten the mood.

"It would appear that you have decided to forgive me for the rude and uncharitable things that I accused you of last April," Elizabeth said, raising an eyebrow.

As Mr. Darcy took a step backward he became aware of several things at once. The first was the presence of a man and woman, standing a few paces away, staring at them. The next were several servants a stone's throw away that had also stopped to stare in stunned silence (though they quickly returned to their duties when they realized they had been discovered). Lastly, he realized that Elizabeth *had kissed him back.*

This last revelation almost propelled him to embrace her once again, but the not so subtle throat clearing of the gentleman a few paces away forestalled him.

"Excuse me, Miss Bennet," Mr. Darcy said. Then, trying to grasp anything to talk about, he settled on her companions, asking for an introduction.

The introductions were made, with much less embarrassment than might be expected under the circumstances. Mr. Darcy invited Mr. and Mrs. Gardiner inside for refreshment and a discussion. Although it was clear they would have to talk about the way Mr. Darcy had greeted their niece, the Gardiners decided it would be best to have the conversation out of sight. As Mr. Darcy had just arrived, it was decided that they would continue their tour of the grounds while he refreshed himself.

And so, Elizabeth found herself following the tour of the Pemberley grounds without the ability to absorb anything that she saw. Evidently, Mr. Darcy still cared for her. Although this knowledge gave her pleasure, she could not forget the manner of his proposal. Her opinion of him had changed dramatically over the previous months, but if he still held her family in disdain, would it matter? She could not marry him if he could not respect her or her family.

Elizabeth had been so oblivious to her surroundings that she was surprised to find Mr. Darcy standing before her. After hurriedly changing out of his travelling clothes he had rushed out to meet them while they were touring the grounds.

He tried to tell himself he was just being a good host, but knew that he was trying to reassure himself that it really had not been a dream. His Elizabeth had truly shown up at Pemberley. Now, he needed to do what he could to keep her there. Permanently.

"Mrs. Reynolds will have some refreshments waiting for us," Mr. Darcy said, while boldly claiming her hand and placing it on his arm.

"She is a very devoted servant," Elizabeth replied. "She could not praise you enough while we toured your home."

"And what do you think of Pemberley?" he asked.

After a couple of false starts, Elizabeth finally laughed then said, "I find myself completely amazed at the warmth of our reception. I can no longer fault Miss Bingley in her attentions to you if she has ever been received in your home in the same manner."

Darcy blushed, as expected, then admitted he had never had the inclination to greet Miss Bingley, or anyone else, in the same manner that he had welcomed Elizabeth when he found her visiting his home. He looked behind him, noticing that Elizabeth's aunt and uncle had tactfully held back a few paces to allow them the opportunity for a semi-private conversation.

"I know that we have much to talk about," Darcy continued, "but I need you to know that I did not intend to place you in such an awkward situation. I think it is clear that I still care for you, but I am learning to care more about the feelings of others, especially yours. I do not want to compel you into a marriage that is not your desire. I am trying to become the gentleman that I always should have been."

Elizabeth found herself completely at a loss for words, a situation that was very rare, indeed.

Chapter 2

As Darcy and Elizabeth approached the house, a quick glance behind revealed that her Aunt and Uncle Gardiner had fallen much further behind than they had realized. Darcy was unsure if the separation was provided as a chance for him and Elizabeth to come to an understanding about how to proceed after their kiss, or if the Gardiners had just needed time to talk things over as well. Not wanting to waste an opportunity, Darcy escorted Elizabeth inside, where a few light refreshments were waiting.

Darcy led Elizabeth to a seat, then prepared a plate for her from the refreshments provided. He was not certain what she would prefer, so provided her a little of everything. As he handed her the plate she let out a little laugh.

"I hope you do not expect me to eat all of this," she said. "Although I am sure it is very good, I do not think I have room for it all."

"I have to admit that I spent much more time staring at your eyes than what you chose to partake of during our acquaintance," Mr. Darcy said with a smile. "I am not sure what you prefer, and I do not want you to dislike my selection. I will pay closer attention in the future."

"I have to admit that I am surprised at your desire to continue our acquaintance," Elizabeth admitted. "After the things I said to you in April, I did not expect to ever have the pleasure of your company again."

"If I remember correctly, at the time you did not find any pleasure in my company," he replied. "Not that I blame you. I behaved most abominably. As I have reflected on things that you said to me I could not help but give your words justice. At least you chose to dislike me for my actions instead of holding the actions of my relations against me. After all, you have met my Aunt Catherine. You know that we all have relations that do not behave as we might wish them to. It does not mean that we love our relations any less, we have just grown accustomed to the foibles in our own family."

"And do you think you could ever become accustomed to the foibles in my family? Could you ever respect them?" Elizabeth held her breath as she waited for a response.

"I have already rebuked myself many times for not giving them the respect that they deserve," he replied. "Your family has been instrumental in shaping the woman that I love. How can I feel anything but gratitude for them?"

Elizabeth realized that there were tears threatening to spill from the corners of her eyes. She reached for a handkerchief, but Darcy was faster. Instead of offering it to her, though, he gently wiped her tears away himself.

"What have I said to make you sad?" he asked quietly.

"Nothing," she replied. "I am not sad, just overwhelmed. It is hard for me to realize just how badly I misjudged you. After reading your letter I realized you were not the man that I thought you were. Now, I realize you are even more kind and caring than I realized."

"You did not misjudge me that badly," Darcy replied. "What did you say of me, that I did not deserve? For, though your accusations were ill-founded, formed on mistaken premises, my behavior to you at the time had merited the severest reproof. It was unpardonable. I cannot think of it without abhorrence."

Secure in the knowledge that Mr. Darcy was indeed repentant for the manner in which he had proposed, and the opinions he had shared concerning her family and connections, Elizabeth pressed her finger to his lips, effectively silencing him.

"Please Mr. Darcy, you must learn some of my philosophy. Think only of the past as its remembrance gives you pleasure."

Darcy pressed a gentle kiss against the finger that was holding his lips in silence then claimed her hand with his own before she could pull it away.

"As I attempt to adopt that philosophy, I can promise that I will always treasure this day," he told her. "This day has brought me more pleasure than I thought I would ever have again in my life."

Their tête-à-tête was interrupted by the entrance of Mr. and Mrs. Gardiner. Elizabeth quickly pulled her hand out of Mr. Darcy's grasp. If her aunt or uncle noticed they gave no indication. Less than a minute after their entrance, Mr. Gardiner made a pointed request to have a look at Mr. Darcy's library.

After the men left the room, Elizabeth tried to keep her Aunt's attention on the splendid variety of refreshments available, but to no avail.

"Have you decided when you will be married?" was Madeline Gardiner's first question.

Elizabeth choked a little on the spice cake. Blushing profusely, she looked toward the window while taking a small sip of tea.

"We did not mean to leave you alone for so much time," Mrs. Gardiner confessed. "You must remember that I am a much slower walker than you. I can only hope you chose to spend the time you had to discuss your upcoming wedding plans. You will not be alone with him again until after the wedding."

"We are not yet engaged," Elizabeth protested.

"My dear, he kissed you in front of your relations and his entire staff," Mrs. Gardiner said. "You can most assuredly consider yourself engaged."

Edward Gardiner was studying the man standing in front of him in the Pemberley library. He did not want to force an engagement, but knew it was essential that it occurred. He was hoping the two young people had been able to come to an understanding in the few minutes they had alone. The whole situation would be much more uncomfortable if it were not for the way Lizzy had reacted when Mr. Darcy had kissed her. If she had immediately tried to push Mr. Darcy away, he would have been concerned about any resultant gossip, but would have allowed his niece to deny an engagement if that was what she desired. As it stood, it was clear that, although she had been surprised by the kiss, she was also a willing participant. In the end he decided a straight forward question would be the best way to begin.

"Have you and Lizzy come to an understanding?" he asked.

"Not yet," Mr. Darcy replied. The blush that had been developing under the silent eye of Mr. Gardiner suddenly deepened in intensity.

"You had at least 15 minutes to yourselves after arriving back at the house," Mr. Gardiner said. "If you were not coming to an understanding, may I ask what you were doing?" A hint of steel had crept its way into Mr. Gardiner's voice.

"We were talking, nothing more," Darcy replied. "I do not know how much of our history together your niece has chosen to share with you, but there were many things we needed to discuss before I felt comfortable asking for her hand."

"You should have thought about that before you accosted her on your lawn," Mr. Gardiner replied. "The only reason we did not have this conversation immediately following your actions was to shield my niece from the embarrassment of the watching servants. Was this the first time you kissed Elizabeth?"

"Yes!" Mr. Darcy exclaimed. "I would never have presumed to kiss her without her permission."

"Then why did you this time?"

"I thought it was a dream," Mr. Darcy confessed quietly, the blush deepening once again.

"And do you dream about my niece often?"

"Every night," Darcy confessed quietly.

"How long have you loved her?" Mr. Gardiner asked after a slight pause.

"Almost from the moment I met her."

Elizabeth had taken to pacing. She was vacillating between concern for her uncle and concern for Mr. Darcy. She knew they were probably not having a pleasant conversation. Her pacing was interrupted at the sound of the door. Her uncle was the first one through the door, and he smiled at her before joining his wife. When Mr. Darcy entered the room he went immediately to Elizabeth's side, then drew her as far away from the Gardiners as possible within the confines of the room. He positioned himself so that he was shielding her from the view of her aunt and uncle.

"I am afraid this is the closest we will come to privacy for some time," Mr. Darcy said. "But there is something that I must ask you."

Elizabeth looked into his eyes, and seeing nothing but love and concern she nodded her head.

"I love you, with my whole soul I love you. Will you do me the honor of becoming my wife?"

"Yes," was all that Elizabeth was able to get out before tears were pouring down her face. As Darcy handed her his handkerchief she tried to explain that she very rarely cried. Whether Darcy believed her or not is unimportant. He was much more concerned with the smile that had filled her face, and the sparkle that had filled her eyes.

Chapter 3

Elizabeth was nervous. The morning after she became engaged to Mr. Darcy, she could be found pacing her dressing room in the Inn at Lambton. It was such a relief to have things out in the open with Darcy, but his sister and the Bingleys would be arriving at Pemberley this day. Fitzwilliam had promised he would come and visit, but he wanted to wait until after his sister arrived to determine whether or not she would come with him. She was quite amazed at her own discomposure; but amongst other causes of disquiet, she dreaded lest the partiality of the brother should have said too much in her favor; and, more than commonly anxious to please, she naturally suspected that every power of pleasing would fail her.

The sound of a carriage drew her to the window, where she saw Fitzwilliam and a lady in a curricle. She wanted to make a good impression before Fitzwilliam told his sister of their engagement. They had agreed the day before that he would wait until Georgiana had met Elizabeth to tell her they had come to an understanding. They were also to wait until Elizabeth's father could be formally asked for her hand before the engagement would be generally announced.

Miss Darcy and her brother appeared, and this formidable introduction took place. With astonishment did Elizabeth see that her new acquaintance was at least as much embarrassed as herself. Since her being at Lambton, she had heard that Miss Darcy was exceedingly proud; but the observation of a very few minutes convinced her that she was only exceedingly shy. She found it difficult to obtain even a word from her beyond a monosyllable.

They had not long been together before Mr. Darcy told her that Bingley was also coming to wait on her; and she had barely time to express her satisfaction, and prepare for such a visitor, when Bingley's quick step was heard on the stairs, and in a moment he entered the room. He inquired in a friendly, though general way, after her family. He tried to give the impression of the same good-humored ease that he had ever done, but Elizabeth was left feeling as if something was lacking. She could not define what was different in his manner, but easily put it out of her mind as she conversed with Georgiana.

Their visitors stayed with them above half-an-hour; and when they arose to depart, Mr. Darcy called on his sister to join him in expressing their wish of seeing Mr. and Mrs. Gardiner, and Miss Bennet, to dinner at Pemberley, before they left the country. Miss Darcy, though with a diffidence which marked her little in the habit of giving invitations, readily obeyed. Mrs. Gardiner readily engaged their attendance for the day after the next.

It had been settled in the evening between the aunt and the niece, that such a striking civility as Miss Darcy's in coming to see them on the very day of her arrival at Pemberley, for she had reached it only to a late breakfast, ought to be imitated, though it could not equaled, by some exertion of politeness on their side; and, consequently, that it would be highly expedient to wait on her at Pemberley the following morning. They were, therefore, to go. Elizabeth was pleased.

When Elizabeth and Mrs. Gardiner arrived at Pemberley they were shown through the hall into the saloon. They were received by Georgiana, with her companion, Mrs. Annesley, as well as Caroline Bingley and Mrs. Hurst.

The delight that infused Georgiana's eyes at their entrance made it clear that her brother had related the news of their engagement. She immediately drew Elizabeth to her side, and a little away from the others. It was clear Miss Bingley was not pleased, but was unsure how to fix the situation as Georgiana and Elizabeth were now situated far enough away to make conversation inconvenient.

When a selection of cold meats and fruits were delivered by a contingent of servants, Caroline decided to make her move. After selecting a variety of refreshments, she made her way to the area of the room where Georgiana and Elizabeth were ensconced. At her appearance, though, Georgiana withdrew back into herself. She had yet to develop the confidence to converse with someone when she was unsure of the hidden meaning behind most of what was said. She did not want to mistakenly give Caroline Bingley any encouragement.

Caroline was not satisfied at all with the trend of the conversation. Elizabeth seemed to be completely unruffled by any enquiries after her family or connections. It was not long before Mr. Darcy entered the room and joined them as well. At first, Caroline hoped he had ventured to their side of the room for her sake, but the blushing looks of pleasure exchanged between Darcy and Elizabeth made it clear whose company he was seeking.

Having never been one to watch her tongue, in the imprudence of anger, Caroline took the first opportunity to make an illusion to Mr. Wickham. Had she known the pain she was causing Miss Darcy, she might have been able to curb her tongue. Had she been aware of the uncharitable thoughts that would run through Mr. Darcy's mind, she would have been stunned silent; which would have been better for all involved.

Aware of the immediate change in Georgiana, and hoping to relieve the discomfort, Elizabeth asked if Georgiana might show her the music room, expressing an interest in a closer look at the pianoforte Darcy had recently acquired for her.

"I'm sorry," Elizabeth said after they were safely ensconced in the music room. "If I had not shown such approval for... a certain member of the militia then Miss Bingley would never have mentioned them in hopes to distract your brother. I can assure you it has been some time since I have had any feelings of generosity toward the militia that was recently stationed in Meryton."

"Do you know? About me and that man?" Georgiana asked quietly.

"Yes," Elizabeth replied. "Your brother explained it to me some time ago."

"What you must think of me," Georgiana replied, lowering her eyes in shame.

"I think you are a very compassionate young lady who was deceived by a charming young man that you had no reason to think ill of," Elizabeth replied. "You had no reason to suspect anything untoward from the man you had always considered a friend. I'm afraid that when men try to protect us from the unpleasant aspects of life they also leave us vulnerable to the machinations of those with less virtuous intentions."

"But I should have known better than to agree to an elopement," Georgiana replied.

"Maybe, but flattery can be a very powerful way to manipulate others," Elizabeth said. "And I believe that the man we are discussing has been practicing the art of flattery for a very long time. I think it is well past time for you to stop dwelling on the past. You have obviously learned from your mistake. You have so much of your life ahead of you. Do not let one evil man keep you from finding joy in life."

It was not long after this discussion that Mrs. Gardiner came in search of her niece. They were due to share dinner with some of Mrs. Gardiner's acquaintances and it was time to return to the inn.

How long Mr. Darcy stood watching the Gardiner carriage make
its way down the lane was unimportant. The look in his eyes
when he returned to his company made it clear, to all those who
chose to accept it, that the object dear to Darcy's heart had left
with the carriage.

The following morning found Fitzwilliam and Georgiana Darcy
making their way to the Inn at Lambton. Although they could not
leave their guests for long, most of their party could be expected
to keep to their beds for the better part of the morning. The
Gardiners had made it clear he should not call on Elizabeth
alone, and Georgiana was more than happy to accompany him.

They were shocked when they were led into the sitting room to
find a very distressed Elizabeth. After Darcy sent the servant in
search of the Gardiners, he bade Elizabeth to sit. Georgiana sat
next to her, holding her hands in comfort. Darcy fumbled around
the room, trying to provide her with something to relieve her
distress, but everything was refused.

"There is nothing the matter with me. I am quite well; I am only
distressed by some dreadful news which I have just received
from Longbourn."

She burst into tears as she alluded to it, and for a few minutes
could not speak another word. Darcy, in wretched suspense,
could only say something indistinctly of his concern, and observe
her in compassionate silence. At length she spoke again. "I have
just had a letter from Jane, with such dreadful news. It cannot be
concealed from anyone. My younger sister has left all her
friends--has eloped; has thrown herself into the power of--of Mr.
Wickham. They are gone off together from Brighton. You know
him too well to doubt the rest. She has no money, no
connections, nothing that can tempt him to--she is lost forever."

While Elizabeth expounded on her feelings of guilt for not protecting her sister from Mr. Wickham, Darcy was silently blaming himself.

Elizabeth found herself explaining all that had been related in the letters. As Darcy's face grew more and more grave, Elizabeth felt her spirits sinking lower and lower. As she finished explaining that the family was hoping Mr. Gardiner would be able to assist in the search, she fell into silent misery.

Darcy nodded his head in silent acquiescence.

It was Georgiana who eventually broke the silence.

"What are you thinking, brother?" she asked. "You know it is hard to interpret your feelings correctly when you have that awful scowl upon your face."

Darcy looked up in surprise. He had almost forgotten the presence of Elizabeth and Georgiana as he was contemplating the best action to take. One look at the worry that was evident in both their eyes, and he brought himself back toward the two women he cared about most in the world.

"I am sorry if I am disturbing you," he said. "I have just been contemplating the best way to go about finding them. You need not distress yourself. I will rectify this problem."

"So, you are not trying to think of a way out of our engagement?" Elizabeth asked tentatively.

The look that filled Darcy's eyes at her question would have been response enough, but he gave a verbal reply, nonetheless.

"Elizabeth, I thought I was clear. I love you. Nothing that Wickham does will change that."

"But, what about what my sister has done?"

"It only concerns me because of the distress it gives you," Darcy replied. "You are not responsible for the actions of your sister."

"What are you planning to do?" Georgiana asked. She had not forgotten her brother's comment indicating he would 'rectify the problem.'

"I will go to London and do what I can to discover them," Darcy replied matter-of-factly. "Because of our history, there is a reasonable chance I will be able to pick up their trail with greater ease than Mr. Bennet or Mr. Gardiner."

"You would do that for me?" Elizabeth asked.

"Yes, but I do have one favor to ask," Darcy replied. "Please do not tell your family of my involvement."

"But, why? They will be grateful for the help," Elizabeth replied.

"I do not want your family to be made uncomfortable with the knowledge that your sister's elopement has passed outside your family circle. I have not yet talked to your father. He does not know that I will very soon be family. He does not need the mortification of knowing that you have shared this with me."

"You are much too good for me, Fitzwilliam," Elizabeth replied.

The Gardiners returned to the Inn as quickly as possible. When they entered the sitting room they were surprised to find Mr. Darcy pacing in the parlor while Elizabeth and Georgiana were in Elizabeth's room, packing Elizabeth's trucks as quickly as possible.

"What is going on here?" Mr. Gardiner asked, trying not to jump to conclusions. After all, it would be unlikely that Darcy would bring his sister or send a servant in search of them if he meant to spirit their niece away.

"I believe these letters from Miss Bennet will explain everything," Mr. Darcy replied, handing the Gardiners the letters from Jane.

They stood in stunned silence while reading the staggering news.

"Do you know what has been written of here?" Mr. Gardiner asked.

"Yes," Darcy replied. "But you can be assured of my secrecy. I would do nothing to hurt Elizabeth or her family."

Elizabeth felt trapped at Longbourn. It had been a week since they had hurried home. Her Uncle Gardiner had only stayed long enough to ensure there was no word from Mr. Bennet before continuing on to London. Her father was in London looking for Lydia. Even Mr. Darcy had joined in the search, though she was unable to talk about his involvement. She did not know if Darcy had told her aunt and uncle of his plans, so did not want to broach the subject. They had not said anything to lead her to believe they knew, and since Darcy had asked her to conceal his actions from her family, she had to assume that meant her aunt and uncle as well.

Deciding to walk off her frustrations, she set out on a ramble through the woods. She had not made it far before she spotted a lone horseman making his way slowly toward her home. She soon recognized the horseman as her father and rushed out to meet him. The despondent look in his eyes forestalled her enquires. It was clear Lydia had not yet been found.

When Mr. Bennet realized his second eldest daughter had seen him, he did his best to conceal his pain. He had never before felt like such a failure as a father. Lydia and Wickham had now been missing for such a length of time that it was clear they would need to be married if they were ever found, no matter how little happiness was likely to result for his daughter. Seeing the sorrow and compassion in Elizabeth's eyes as she watched him approach, he swore to himself he would be a more diligent father. He would not let another man force any of his daughters into matrimony.

Chapter 4

Elizabeth could not forget the look of pain she had briefly witnessed in her father's face when he first returned to Longbourn. He had quickly composed his features, and tried to make light of the grief he was feeling, but it was clear to his eldest two daughters that he was in pain.

Two days after Mr. Bennet's return to Longbourn they were relieved of the greatest of their anxiety by an express from Mr. Gardiner indicating that Lydia and Wickham had been found. He gave a brief explanation of the settlement that would be required to ensure the wedding was performed. Although there was much to lament, the postscript at the end of the missive caused him even greater sorrow, and had him sending a servant in search of his second daughter. He was not incredibly pleased when both Jane and Lizzy returned to his study.

After relating all the contents of the letter that applied to Lydia, he sent Jane away with all but the last page of the express to share with their mother. When Lizzy made to follow Jane from the room, Mr. Bennet called her back, indicating there was a matter he wished to discuss with her in private.

"Your uncle included information on another matter that, it appears, will also need my attention in the very near future," Mr. Bennet began. "It would appear you had quite an interesting visit to Mr. Darcy's home while touring Derbyshire."

Not wanting to give anything away that her father did not already know, Elizabeth asked him what her Uncle Gardiner had related.

"He has said enough to make it clear they believe there will be a wedding between Mr. Darcy and yourself in the very near future," he replied. "They expect Mr. Darcy will be on my doorstep within the next few days expecting to be granted your hand in marriage."

"Yes, I expect that to be the case," Elizabeth replied.

Misinterpreting the meaning behind the tears that sprung to Elizabeth's eyes, he tried to console her by saying: "Do not fear, my dear. After this mess with Lydia, any mention of a kiss between you and Mr. Darcy can be easily written off as gossip. Derbyshire is so far away, I find in highly unlikely we will ever hear of it again. When Mr. Darcy arrives I will assure him that he need not trouble himself with the thought that he will ever see you again."

"But I will know it is not gossip," Elizabeth replied. "Aunt and Uncle Gardiner will know it is not gossip, and many of his servants will also know it is not gossip."

Mr. Bennet closed his eyes. This was not something that he wanted to hear.

"I think we can trust your aunt and uncle not to spread the tale," Mr. Bennet replied. "As far as Mr. Darcy's servants are concerned, it will be up to him to stem the tide of their tales. In the past he has always made his dislike clear. Although I cannot imagine why he would suddenly decide to kiss you, I can only imagine he will be relieved to be released from your engagement."

"But he does not dislike me," Elizabeth exclaimed, trying valiantly (but failing) to fight the tears in her eyes. "He does not want to be released from our engagement. It is not the first time he has asked me."

Lost to her emotions, Elizabeth had not meant to share that last piece of news with her father. She momentarily hoped that her crying would have made it impossible for him to understand her, but the look on his face made it clear that it was not the case.

"Why is this the first time I am hearing of this?" he asked.

"I did not accept his first proposal."

"And when was this proposal made?"

"Before leaving Kent."

There was silence in the room for several minutes before Mr. Bennet could compose his thoughts into a rational argument.

"Let me see if I have this straight," he began. "While in Kent, Mr. Darcy proposed, but you refused him. The next time you had the opportunity to see him is while touring the grounds of his home, at which time he kissed you in front of others, thereby ensuring an acceptance to his proposal." With a reluctant nod from Elizabeth, he continued. "There is nothing further you can say that would tempt me to grant such a controlling and manipulative man your hand in marriage."

"But you do not understand," Elizabeth said. "My feelings for him have changed so dramatically that even if he had not kissed me I would have accepted his hand if he were to offer it again."

"How?" Mr. Bennet asked. "You did not have the pleasure of continuing his acquaintance after his first proposal. How has your opinion changed so drastically?"

Feeling that revealing the impropriety of accepting a letter from Mr. Darcy would not help her case in any way, she chose not to reveal its existence. As she tried to think of a way to explain the drastic change of her feelings without revealing her letter, she sat in her chair crying. After she had opened and closed her mouth a few times with no sound coming out, her father decided that he had had enough.

"Lizzy, I know you are trying to spare my feelings. You do not want to be the cause of an additional scandal being brought upon our family. I appreciate your efforts, but I assure you that nothing will induce me to give Mr. Darcy permission to make you his bride. I will not see you settled in a marriage where you are unable to respect your husband simply because he has acted so incredibly high-handedly to try and force your hand. When he arrives I will see him then send him on his way. You need not even speak with him. I will handle everything."

During this speech Mr. Bennet had risen from his chair and approached his daughter. Meaning to comfort her, he placed his hand on her shoulder, but was surprised at the result. Elizabeth flinched away, looked at her father dejectedly, and then ran from the room.

To say that Mrs. Bennet was completely unaware of the turmoil surrounding her second daughter would be an understatement. She was so caught up with joy at the news that Lydia would be married (and to an officer no less!) that she was not even aware when Elizabeth did not join the family for dinner that night, nor breakfast the next morning.

Jane was not so oblivious.

After watching her closest sister stop by the kitchen for a small breakfast that she could take with her into the prettyish kind of little wilderness to the side of the lawn, Jane decided it was time to find out what was troubling Elizabeth. She was surprised to find her sitting directly on the ground, picking absently at her food, with a look of despondency in her eyes. Growing up with Lizzy, she was accustomed to seeing a wide variety of emotions cross her sisters face. She was passionate by nature, and much more inclined to fits of joy or anger. Never before had Jane seen her sister with such a dejected look.

"Dearest Lizzy, whatever is the matter?" Jane asked. "It almost seems you have become more despondent now that Lydia has been found, instead of allowing yourself the relief that is felt by the rest of the family."

Elizabeth shifted her gaze so that she was staring at Jane.

"I am not thinking of Lydia at all," Elizabeth confessed.

"What else could possibly cause such sorrow?"

"Father has told me he will refuse his consent to the man I am planning to marry."

Jane joined her sister on the ground, encouraging Elizabeth to lean against her before she continued.

"Did he give a reason for his refusal?"

"He thinks he is doing me a favor. He is certain that I will be unable to respect my husband."

Jane did not want to push her sister's confidence, and although she was not much of a gossip by nature, she had to admit that she was incredibly curious as to identity of the gentleman they were discussing. Try as she might, she could not conjure up a name to go with this mysterious gentleman whom Elizabeth had apparently agreed to marry. She started rubbing her sisters back consolingly, ruling out every gentleman she could think of, for the mere fact that they had not had any callers besides their Aunt Phillips since Lizzy had returned to Longbourn.

"Why does our father fear you will be unable to respect this gentleman?" she finally asked, hoping for some sort of clue. After all, how could she help her sister if she did not know all the particulars?

"He will not accept that I no longer dislike him," Elizabeth replied.

"Who?" Jane finally asked, unable to contain her curiosity.

Elizabeth opened her mouth to answer, but before any words came out the beating of a horse's hooves could be heard on the drive. Jumping up, Elizabeth left the remains of her forgotten breakfast on the ground to try and catch a glimpse of the caller. The combined look of excitement and misery on Elizabeth's face told Jane that this was the gentleman they had been discussing. Turning in the direction of the gentleman, she was overcome with confusion. *Hadn't Lizzy told her she had refused Mr. Darcy?*

Fitzwilliam Darcy knew it was probably still early for callers, but he had made good time from London and wanted nothing more than to see Elizabeth. The last week had been torture. Searching for Wickham had been inconvenient, but was nothing compared to being separated from Lizzy now that she had agreed to become his wife.

As he approached Longbourn, he was surprised by the sight of a clearly distraught Elizabeth rushing toward him. He quickly reigned in his horse so he could dismount and gather her in his arms. He was so intent on comforting Elizabeth, he was unaware of Jane's presence at the opening in the hedgerow from whence Elizabeth appeared.

"What is the matter, dearest?" Darcy asked softly into Elizabeth's ear.

"My father does not believe that I have grown to love you," she replied. "He thinks the only reason I am marrying you is because you kissed me. He is planning on refusing his consent."

Darcy was speechless. Although he had done much to mend his ways since his initial proposal, he was still a man that was not used to being denied anything for which he asked. This was not an obstacle that he was anticipating. He tilted Elizabeth's face towards his own so that he could see her eyes.

"What do you want me to do?" he asked.

"Please, try to convince him," she replied. "Maybe he will be more open to the match than he was yesterday. Either way, when you are done, I will be waiting out here for you. Come and find me, no matter what my father says."

With a nod, he prepared to release Elizabeth and face her father. He was pleasantly surprised when Elizabeth reached up on her tiptoes to whisper "I love you Fitzwilliam" before giving him a quick peck on the cheek and running back into the hedgerows

.

Chapter 5

Fitzwilliam Darcy was surprised to be received at the entrance to Longbourn by none other than Elizabeth's father, Mr. Bennet. Elizabeth had just revealed to him the fact that her father was planning on refusing his consent to their marriage. Although this concerned him greatly, there was in fact a look of heartfelt delight infusing his face. Elizabeth had just revealed to him that she loved him. It was the first time she had spoken those words. She had responded most favorably when he had kissed her. She had indicated that her feelings for him had undergone a great change from the time of his first proposal. She had even agreed to marry him. But, up until that morning she had not yet uttered those words that made everything right in the world.

Darcy followed Mr. Bennet to his study, quickly finding himself facing his host across his desk. Instead of looking directly at Darcy, Mr. Bennet stared out the window of his study.

"I have had a very trying few weeks," Mr. Bennet admitted. "To top it all off, when I tried to comfort my second daughter, assuring her that she would not have to marry a man that would have the audacity to kiss her in front of her relations after she had previously refused his offer of marriage, she ran from me. Then, while sitting here, contemplating why she would do such a thing, I witnessed her approaching you on your arrival for a quick word before running back into the hedgerows." After a few minutes of quiet, Mr. Bennet continued, "I consider myself a reasonably intelligent man. I cannot help but think there is something I am not being told."

"I do not know what Elizabeth has told you," Darcy replied hesitantly. "I can assure you that I love your daughter desperately. When she refused me while I was visiting my aunt in Kent I was crushed. It was not until getting back to my rooms that I realized how rude I had been while trying to propose. I had not originally intended on proposing to her that evening, and I blurted out the first thing that came to my head. It was not very flattering. When she was justifiably offended and leveled her other accusations against me, I was too upset to realize the implications of everything that I said. With a cooler head, I attempted to meet with her the next morning to defend myself against her accusations. Over the next few months I saw her everywhere I went, even though she was not there."

Darcy paused; trying to decide whether or not to admit just how lost he had been when he found Elizabeth wandering the grounds of Pemberley. Mr. Bennet could tell that this young man was experiencing some turmoil while relating his tale, but he was not inclined to relieve him. So, they sat there in silence, Mr. Bennet staring down the young man fidgeting in his study, waiting for him to finish.

"I was tortured during the day with illusive sights of her, while greeting her every night in my dreams as if she had consented to be my wife. I had envisioned her coming out to meet me on my return to Pemberley so many times, that when I saw her there I reacted as I did in my dreams." Darcy paused once again. "I thought I had lost her forever, but then I realized I was not dreaming, and that she had returned my embrace. I do not think I can describe to you the joy and confusion that I experienced at that moment. When she dashed away my confusion and agreed to marry me I became the happiest of men."

Silence once again reigned in Mr. Bennet's study. He could not doubt that Mr. Darcy loved his daughter Elizabeth, but he was still unhappy with the circumstances. He wanted some assurances that Elizabeth truly loved Darcy. He did not want her to accept him simply because of the way she had reacted when he had kissed her. A happy marriage required much more than a passing infatuation. Elizabeth needed to be reminded of Mr. Darcy's opinions of her family and friends. She needed to be reminded of why she disliked him so much in the first place.

"I do not doubt that you love my Lizzy very much," Mr. Bennet said slowly. "However, I am not yet ready to give my consent to this match. I am not yet convinced that Lizzy loves you as she ought. As you are aware, Lizzy can be quite stubborn and set on getting her own way. I do not want to drive you to do anything rash. I do not think I could survive if Lizzy ran away right now." After a slight pause, he continued, "I do not know if you are aware, but Elizabeth will be twenty-one in just over two months, at which time you will no longer need my consent to legally wed. Due to the warning from my brother Gardiner that the two of you should not remain unchaperoned at any time, I do not feel it would be prudent for you to stay with us at Longbourn. If you will secure for yourself other lodgings and stay in the area until Lizzy comes of age, then I will give my blessing to your marriage if that is what she still desires. I only ask that you wait until after her birthday to make any announcements. As I have not given my consent, nothing can be made official until after she is of age."

"So, you will not deny me access to Elizabeth?" Darcy asked. "You will let me see her during the next two months?"

"Yes, in fact I insist upon it," came the reply. "Find lodgings as soon as may be, and come to visit as often as you like. I expect Elizabeth will want you to join us at all our social obligations over the next couple of months. Just remember that you are not to visit with Elizabeth without a chaperone. Either her mother or one of her sisters must be with you constantly. At the end of two months, if she still wants to marry you, I will give you my blessing."

Darcy was disappointed and elated at the same time. He would wish to have Elizabeth as his bride as soon as possible, and chafed at the two month delay before announcements could be sent out and plans could be made. At the same time, Mr. Bennet was allowing him to come and visit with Elizabeth. He would not be cut off from the woman that he loved.

"Thank you, sir," Darcy said. "I would not want to face another separation from Elizabeth, especially now that I know she loves me in return. Even though you are unhappy with the prospect of my marriage to your daughter, thank you for not denying me the ability to visit her."

"One more thing," Mr. Bennet replied. "Please remember that you are not yet officially engaged. You should not be calling her Elizabeth."

With a blush, Darcy consented to refer to her as the much more proper 'Miss Elizabeth.'

After watching Mr. Darcy enter their home, Jane had finally convinced Elizabeth to relate the tale of her engagement. Thankful for the understanding ear, Elizabeth proceeded to admit to Jane that her feelings for Darcy had begun to change after recognizing the merit in his letter. After having several weeks to contemplate her changed opinion, she happened to tour Pemberley with her Aunt and Uncle Gardiner. While there, Mrs. Reynolds, the housekeeper, lavished such praise on Mr. Darcy that she could not help but have a better opinion of the man. Mentioning the kiss only in passing, Elizabeth related some details of their subsequent conversation, and how she came to realize he was truly the most caring and loving man of her acquaintance. Her heart now engaged, when he asked her to marry him she could do naught but agree.

While relating her tale, Elizabeth calmed down considerably. It made her wonder why she did not go to Jane immediately the previous evening and pour out her troubles. Jane had always been compassionate. As she explained her feelings, she even came to understand them better herself. She hoped that this greater understanding would enable her to express her wishes to her father much more rationally.

Jane had just succeeded in coaxing a laugh from Elizabeth (with a splendid impersonation of their mother in the event she was to be told of Elizabeth's engagement) when they heard footsteps approaching. Expecting Darcy to return at any moment, Elizabeth turned in the direction of the footsteps with a look of expectation on her face. She was surprised to find that her father had accompanied her beloved. While she tried to decide whether or not this was a good sign, she looked into Darcy's face, looking for some clues. What she saw there gave her such great relief that she flew at her father, hugging him tightly.

"Thank you, Papa," Elizabeth said.

"I think you are a bit too hasty," Mr. Bennet replied with a slight laugh to cover his discomfort. "Wait until you hear what is to be said."

Elizabeth backed away a few steps, and Jane walked to her side, grasping her hand in support. They both then turned to Darcy for an explanation.

"Your father has not given his consent," Darcy admitted. "He has asked that we take the next two months until you come of age. At that time he will give us his blessing."

Although the information was presented very quickly, Elizabeth found herself experiencing a variety of emotion at his words. As the last words registered, she smiled widely, first at Darcy then at her father.

"There are a couple of circumstances that Darcy has yet to relate," Mr. Bennet said. "He will be expected to find lodgings in the area so that you have the opportunity to see him regularly, but you are never to see each other without a chaperone. Also, I may not be able to legally stop you from getting married after your birthday, but I will only give you my blessing if you are still able to assure me that you want to marry Mr. Darcy at that time. I have also asked that any mention of an engagement wait until that time, as you do not have my consent."

Elizabeth again threw herself at her father, hugging him tightly.

"Well, I can see that with Jane here you will be sufficiently chaperoned. I will see you at luncheon."

As Mr. Bennet made his way back to the house, Elizabeth walked to Mr. Darcy's side. Both very cognizant of Jane's presence, they refrained from embracing, but Darcy did draw Elizabeth's hand to his mouth for a lingering kiss.

"I will stay at the Inn in Meryton for the next two nights, then I need to return to town for a few days to see some business to completion," Mr. Darcy explained. "When I come back I hope to have permission from Bingley to stay at Netherfield, but even if I do not I will return."

"I'm afraid your guests at Pemberley will not appreciate you desertion," Elizabeth pointed out. "If you must return to them for a visit I would understand."

"No, my sister will understand my reasons for staying away. When I left she gave me every assurance that she would be able to see to our guests until the end of their visit. Since I am not there I would not be surprised to learn that they shortened their visit. Although Bingley does not know all of the particulars, when he learns that we are to be married he will understand."

By this time they had started walking down one of the many paths leading through the woods around Longbourn. Jane was following at a discreet distance, so that if they spoke quietly they would not be overheard.

"Am I correct in assuming your business in London will be completed on the day of my youngest sister's wedding?" she asked him.

"Yes," he replied. "I hate to have to leave you at all, but I have pledged myself to be there."

"Were you the one to find them, then? When my father returned he seemed without hope. If my uncle had any leads I do not think he would have been as despondent."

"Yes, I was able to track him down through Georgiana's old companion, Mrs. Younge. After everything had been arranged I contacted your aunt and uncle. By that time your father had already returned home."

"So, he still does not know of your involvement."

"No, and I would rather keep it that way. I have always felt uncomfortable with others knowing my personal life. I imagine that your father would feel more comfortable with the fewest number of people as possible being aware of Lydia's indiscretion."

"But if he knew, he may relent and let us marry sooner," Elizabeth argued.

"It will only be a two month delay. We can then have the banns read and be married within a month of your birthday. I am willing to wait three months to allow your family their privacy."

After continuing in silence for a few minutes, Elizabeth introduced a new subject.

"If you return to Netherfield, do you think Mr. Bingley is likely to join you?"

After a slightly awkward pause, Mr. Darcy replied:

"It is unlikely he will return to Netherfield until after he is married. Even then, he may choose to not renew the lease."

Another awkward pause, with a glance to make sure that Jane was out of hearing distance.

"Mr. Bingley is engaged?"

"He has been engaged since last September." Another awkward pause. "As I told you in my letter, I have often seen him fall in love. Last summer he decided that all he needed to make the feeling last was some resolve. He proposed to the younger sister of one of our friends from Cambridge. Because of her age, her parents asked that they not mention it until after the end of her first season. The only reason I know is because he had told me he was proposing beforehand, so he told me the result. He hasn't even told his sisters, though it is evident that they suspect something."

"Why did he not say anything? Why did you not tell me in your letter?"

"His intent in leasing Netherfield was establishing a home for his young bride. His intent was to establish himself in the area, making it easier to introduce his bride when the time came. He did not intend to fall in love again. He did not realize he was falling in love until he was half gone. After the Netherfield ball he went to London with the purpose of breaking his engagement so that he could propose to your sister. Since the engagement had not been announced he hoped to break it without any sort of scandal. I followed him to London to convince him that he should honor his commitment. Even though the engagement has not been announced, he had still made a commitment to the young lady. When we were able to convince him that Jane did not care for him, he resigned himself to honor his commitment. I did not tell you about this in my letter because it was not my secret to tell."

Suddenly recalling the subtle warning in Caroline's letter to Jane indicating that they were hoping to soon call Georgiana her sister, Elizabeth felt her stomach drop.

"Is it Georgiana? Is Mr. Bingley engaged to your sister?"

"What? No. What gave you that idea?"

"It was something that Caroline alluded to in her farewell note to Jane."

"Although the girl's name is Georgiana, it is not my sister. She is Georgiana Crawford. Miss Bingley must have overheard part of a conversation between Bingley and myself and drawn her own conclusions. It would actually explain some comments she has made recently."

"So, there really is no hope for Jane and Bingley?"

"I am very sorry to disappoint you. I will always try to give you everything that you want, but I cannot in good conscience encourage Bingley to break his engagement. It should be announced next month."

"I understand, I just feel so bad for dear Jane. I have never seen her so attached to someone before. But I also feel for Miss Crawford. I would feel guilty if Jane's happiness came at someone else's expense. At least I know I *should* feel guilty in such a case."

A muffled sound behind them caused Elizabeth to look behind her. She had not realized Jane had slowly closed the gap between them. She did not know how much Jane had overheard, but the tears in her eyes made it clear she had heard enough.

Chapter 6

With one look at the tears streaming down Jane's face, Elizabeth released her hold on Darcy's arm and folded her sister into a comforting embrace. The look in Elizabeth's eyes as she gazed back on Darcy made it clear that she needed some time alone with her sister. Although Darcy did not want to part from his beloved, he knew that to remain at this point would be selfishness. He needed to give Elizabeth time to condole with Jane.

After Darcy made his excuses, promising to call again the next day, Elizabeth led Jane to a bench along the path where they would have some privacy.

"Dear Jane, you are much too kind. You do not deserve this."

"No, Lizzy. Mr. Bingley never made me a promise. Even though I preferred him above any other gentleman of our acquaintance, I have nothing to reproach him with."

"Does your kindness know no bounds? If it were me, I would not be so forgiving."

"At least now I know why he never came back. I am no longer left wondering. I can move on."

Three days had passed since Mr. Darcy had arrived to ask Mr. Bennet for Elizabeth's hand in marriage. After staying in the area for only a couple of days, Darcy returned to town in order to do his part to ensure the marriage between Lydia and Mr. Wickham.

The Bennet family was now anxiously awaiting the arrival of Mr. and Mrs. Wickham. Darcy had confided in Elizabeth that he would not return until the next day.

The family was gathered in the breakfast room to greet the Wickhams on their arrival, and so to this room Lydia exuberantly made her way as soon as she arrived, with her new husband in tow. The Wickhams were so easy in their entrance, that any casual observer would have no reason to think they had done anything wrong. Mrs. Bennet met them just as enthusiastically, though Mr. Bennet and his three eldest daughters were much more reserved.

As they were going into dinner, Mrs. Bennet could already be heard planning all the dinners and parties they could possibly hold during the ten days her newly married daughter would be with them.

Darcy found himself pacing the halls of Netherfield Park. After the Wickham marriage, he had joined the Gardiners for dinner before preparing to return to Hertfordshire. He had then left London before dawn in order to arrive as soon as possible. Now, he was stuck waiting until the appropriate visiting hour to call on Elizabeth. He kept telling himself that three months was not a long time, but just the half hour stretching out in front of him before he would be able to see Elizabeth again seemed interminable.

He had already instructed the stables to have his horse ready for him at the appropriate time. Ten minutes before he could expect his horse to be prepared he decided to go outside to wait. Only five minutes later his horse was brought around from the stables.

He arrived at Longbourn just shy of the appropriate visiting hour.

When Mr. Darcy was shown into the drawing room, he was a bit surprised at the cold manner in which he was received by Mrs. Bennet, especially after it was clear that she was more than welcoming to the man that had eloped with Lydia.

Wickham had also noticed the cool reception that Mr. Darcy received from Mrs. Bennet, and decided to use it to his advantage. When Mary inevitably shared some strictures from Fordyce's Sermons, Wickham found his chance.

"Miss Mary, your devotion is to be commended," Wickham said. "It must be a great comfort to have the opportunity to study the sermons on a daily basis. I wish that I would have had the same opportunity. Alas, my occupation in the military precludes any chance I have for an in-depth study of the church."

Although Lydia would not have found her husband nearly as engaging if he were dressed as a clergyman instead of in a red coat, she knew it was not a real option, so she readily agreed with the sentiment. As Mrs. Bennet started making pointed references to the person that she felt should have provided a clerical living for her son-in-law, Darcy stood up and made his way to a window. Elizabeth felt all the embarrassment that was incumbent in the situation, and decided to try her best to diffuse it.

"While conversing with an acquaintance from Derbyshire, I heard that there was a time when sermon-making was not so palatable to you as it seems to be at present; that you actually declared your resolution of never taking orders, and that the business had been compromised accordingly."

Wickham had assumed that Darcy's presence at Longbourn was out of a desire to make sure he behaved himself before leaving for his new regiment in the north. He was not aware that Darcy would share any of the particulars of his early life with Elizabeth. He need not have worried, though, as Mrs. Bennet came to his defense before he had a chance to fabricate another half-truth.

"Oh Lizzy, do not be ridiculous," Mrs. Bennet exclaimed. "What intelligent young man would make a compromise that would deny himself the security of a proffered living? I am sure that your new acquaintance is not aware of the true damage that has been done to our poor Wickham." This last was said in a hard tone and a look in the direction of Mr. Darcy.

"On the contrary, Mother," Elizabeth replied. "My acquaintance was intimately involved in the arrangements."

"Please be quiet, Lizzy," Mrs. Bennet admonished. "If you cannot support our dear Wickham then I do not want to hear any more on this subject."

Elizabeth stood with a huff and made her way over to the same window as Mr. Darcy. The conversation quickly flowed onto other topics as Wickham flattered all in the room (except Darcy) and Mrs. Bennet praised the intelligence and wit of her new son-in-law. Elizabeth had never been more mortified by her family.

For her part, Mrs. Bennet still did not understand why Mr. Darcy was visiting at Longbourn. Mr. Bennet had told her to expect him regularly for the next few months, but did not give a reason. As long as he was in their company, she could see no harm in encouraging him to give a living to Wickham.

To all appearances, Elizabeth and Darcy were looking out the window, admiring the view in relative silence. Although they were both facing the window, they were oblivious to everything in front of them. Although her whole body was drawn to his presence, Elizabeth only allowed her eyes to stray to the side, where they saw Darcy staring at her in a similar fashion.

"I am sorry," Elizabeth whispered as quietly as possible.

"You have nothing to apologize for," Darcy whispered back.

"She has no right to treat you this way."

"I am the one that left such a horrible impression while staying in Hertfordshire. It is my fault that Wickham was able to deceive so many with ease."

"You take too much upon yourself. What if you were not here? Do you think anyone would have believed him any less if they had never met you?"

Mary Bennet glanced at her sister Elizabeth. She was accustomed to being overlooked while in the same room as her sisters. She had long reconciled herself to the fact that she was not as beautiful as the others, and had sought her refuge in books. Typically, though, the others were not completely oblivious to her presence. It was clear that neither Elizabeth nor Mr. Darcy realized she was close enough to overhear their whispered conversation.

Mary was also looking for a way out of the room. She was upset that her observations from Fordyce's Sermons that were meant as an admonishment to her youngest sister were twisted around to appear as if she was in support of Mr. Wickham.

"Elizabeth, would you mind taking a turn about the garden with me?" Mary asked. "I believe the roses are blooming and I would like to collect some for my rose water. If I wait until any later in the day they may become wilted."

"Certainly Mary," Elizabeth thankfully replied. "I will just stop by the kitchen and collect some shears."

"Mr. Darcy, you may come as well, if you would like," Mary said.

"Thank you Miss Mary, I believe I shall."

Free from the oppression of the drawing room, Darcy drew Elizabeth's hand to his arm. He was quickly learning that it was easy to be pleasant to Elizabeth's sisters when they were separate. Putting them all in a drawing room together was still very overwhelming.

"Miss Mary, thank you for inviting me on this excursion," said Mr. Darcy. "I must admit I have never had the inclination to collect roses. Perhaps you will be able to teach me what I should be looking for if I were to venture out on my own."

Although Mary had invited Mr. Darcy to join her and Elizabeth, she did not expect him to talk to her. Very few of their acquaintances ever thought to talk to her, and she did not think he would be an exception. Her purpose in inviting him to the garden was to allow him and Elizabeth to continue their conversation with a little more privacy, while also allowing her some distance from Lydia and her husband.

Sensing that Mary was slightly uncomfortable with Mr. Darcy addressing her directly, Elizabeth decided to step in.

"I was not aware you were in need of rose water," Elizabeth said playfully. "I thought it was only ladies who preferred the floral scents. Or, do you plan on preparing some for Georgiana?"

"I doubt I will ever find the need to prepare rose water," Darcy admitted. "Though, there are other reasons to collect the blossoms."

"Surely your gardener would be able to collect any blossoms you require."

"That may be true, but sometimes it has a special meaning when the flowers have been collected personally. When I am married, I hope to be able to provide a fresh bouquet to my wife without the help of my staff."

"But, Mr. Darcy, you would cut the stems for a bouquet much differently than we will be cutting them today for the rose water," Mary said, not noticing the blush on Elizabeth's cheeks.

"Then, you will just have to show me the difference," Mr. Darcy replied. He had noticed Elizabeth's blush and was delighting in it. "Perhaps today I could make a practice bouquet. I will want to be prepared."

Darcy was once again approaching Longbourn. He had enjoyed spending time in the garden with Elizabeth and Miss Mary the day previous. In the end, he had ended up doing most of the cutting for both Miss Mary's rose water and a bouquet for each young woman. By her reaction, he did not think Miss Mary had ever been given flowers before. After they had returned to the house and Miss Mary had taken her bouquet to her room, Elizabeth had even thanked him for thinking of her sister. He had tried to point out that Miss Mary was the one to invite them outside in the first place, and that all the roses came from their gardens, but she had stopped him with a look and a smile.

Now, he had been invited to the first party that Mrs. Bennet had planned to celebrate the recent marriage of her youngest daughter. He was approaching Longbourn with a little bit of apprehension. Wickham seemed to be able to get under his skin at every opportunity. He was not looking forward to a party where Wickham was one of the guests of honor. But, if this was the only way he could be close to Elizabeth until her birthday, then he would be there.

As he approached the stables to hand off his horse, he was surprised to see Wickham just returning from a ride as well.

"Since this party is for you, I would have expected you to be in attendance before any of the guests arrived," Darcy observed.

"Please," Wickham replied sarcastically. "You know you are a quarter hour early. I have arrived in plenty of time to prepare to meet the lovely people of Meryton."

"If you care so little for their company, then why did you come for a visit?"

"I can't very well ignore all the demands of my wife. I believe part of our agreement was that I at least appear to be happy, is that not correct? Although, I must say you were concealing your true motivations in arranging my marriage. If I would have known you had intentions on pursuing Miss Elizabeth I would have asked for more money. I do not doubt you would have done everything in your power to keep her reputation clean." After a slight pause he continued, "Although, this may be even better. If we are to be brothers, I am sure I can count on you to continue helping my career. You would not want your lovely wife's sister to be destitute, now would you?"

"If you think you will be able to continue to count on my money to bail you out, then you are mistaken. Elizabeth is just as disgusted with you as I am. She cares for her sister, but would not encourage me to be generous towards you as she knows you will gamble away any money you receive."

"I'm sure I will be able to persuade her otherwise," Wickham said with a grin. "She is very lively. How long do you think she will be happy married to a man that hides his feelings so deeply? It is only a matter of time until her eyes wander, and I will be sure to be in her line of sight. You know I was able to charm her once. How hard do you think it will be for me to charm her into an indiscretion when she has become bored with you?"

It was unclear whether or not Wickham would have continued to goad Darcy, for Darcy had reached his limit. As Wickham had left Ramsgate without coming face to face with Darcy, he had never had the opportunity to experience his full wrath. He was not expecting Darcy to throw a punch, especially in the view of servants. Darcy's right hook was so quick, that even if Wickham had been expecting it there was little he could have done to deflect it. When Wickham found himself on the ground with a bloody nose, he was quite shocked.

"You just broke my nose!" Wickham yelled in astonishment.

"Actually, I believe your horse was spooked and reared in fright, accidently kicking you in the face," Darcy replied.

"You know very well that is not what happened."

"What did you expect me to do? Just sit there and let you insult me and the woman that I love?" Darcy's voice had taken on an edge of steel. This was a side of Darcy that Wickham had never seen firsthand. He had never been more scared in his life.

"Now," Darcy continued, "you had better get back to the house and clean up. The other guests will be arriving soon."

The stable hands were more than willing to agree to Mr. Darcy's version of how Mr. Wickham received his broken nose, even if Mr. Darcy had not paid them each a couple of shillings. They had overheard much of the discussion preceding the incident. Although Miss Elizabeth was not a regular visitor to the stables, she was still much loved by all of the Longbourn staff. They knew which gentleman deserved their loyalty.

Chapter 7

Mr. Bennet was confused.

When Mr. Darcy had arrived for the dinner party in honor of Mr. and Mrs. Wickham he had immediately taken up a post next to Elizabeth. His face was the inscrutable mask that all were familiar with from Darcy's first introduction to Hertfordshire society. Mr. Bennet was delighted that he was showing his true form so quickly, and looked towards his daughter, Elizabeth, planning on directing her attention to the young man if she had not already noticed his behavior. At this rate, Mr. Bennet was sure he would have Elizabeth freed from Mr. Darcy within a fortnight. She would then be sorry she had not taken her father's advice, they could have a short conversation where all would be forgiven, and they could then continue on in the same way they had always been before Mr. Darcy had intruded on their society. Then, in a few years, she could fall in love with someone that would be more worthy of her (though he had to admit he had never met a man he felt could come close to being worthy of his Lizzy).

Mr. Bennet's glance in Elizabeth's direction revealed that she had indeed noticed Mr. Darcy's mask. Mr. Bennet was confused because instead of reacting with disappointment or annoyance with Mr. Darcy, Elizabeth looked concerned. Concerned for Mr. Darcy. Even though he was behaving in his proud, disagreeable manner.

Mr. Bennet was so stunned that he caught himself staring at the young couple. He was only interrupted at the entrance of his son-in-law. Lydia's squeal attracted every head in the room. It was clear Mr. Wickham had met some sort of unfortunate accident. His nose was swollen, and the beginning of a spectacular bruise was forming.

If Mr. Bennet had succeeded in watching Darcy and Elizabeth while Mr. Wickham told his tale of bravely pulling a young boy out of the way of a rearing horse, he could have gained a little insight. As it was, he was watching those closest to Mr. Wickham as he spread his tale.

Mr. Wickham explained that after dismounting his horse a young boy came scampering out of nowhere. His horse was spooked, and reared up on his hind legs. Seeing the danger the boy was in, Wickham quickly leaped in front of his horse to protect the child. In the process of calming the horse, he was accidently kicked in the face.

Part way through the story, Elizabeth glanced at Mr. Darcy. Realizing he had not been surprised in the least that Mr. Wickham had arrived with a broken nose, she raised one eyebrow in inquiry. At first, Darcy did not respond, but as Wickham painted himself a hero, he finally rolled his eyes and shrugged his shoulders.

When Mr. Bennet finally returned his gaze to Darcy and Elizabeth, Mr. Darcy's mask was firmly in place, but Elizabeth was trying, unsuccessfully, to hide her mirth.

Mrs. Bennet was confused.

Although this might come as a surprise to others, this was a new experience. She had become adept at rationalizing the actions of others to suit her desires. Even if her assumptions were often wrong, she was not left feeling confused. Now, she could not understand why being kicked in the face by a horse would make Mr. Wickham disinclined to talk about the injustices committed by Mr. Darcy.

The previous evening, while retiring for bed, Mrs. Bennet had pondered what could possibly bring Mr. Darcy for an extended visit to Hertfordshire without Mr. Bingley. She convinced herself that Mr. Darcy was visiting them out of respect for the Wickhams. Darcy and Wickham had played together as boys. Now that Mr. Wickham was respectably married to her daughter Lydia, Mrs. Bennet had convinced herself that Mr. Darcy was visiting in an attempt to heal the breach the had arisen between the two young men. *What better way to heal the breach then through offering Mr. Wickham a living. Then, when they are friends again, the girls will be thrown into the paths of other rich men. Jane may even have another chance to win Mr. Bingley.*

Thus had been her thoughts as she time and again tried to bring up the matter, but each time Mr. Wickham deftly changed the subject. By the time the last course had been served, she was actually falling a little out of humour with her new son-in-law. She welcomed the separation of the sexes evening as an opportunity to talk some sense into her daughter, Lydia. If Mr. Wickham could not be relied upon to seize the opportunity, then surely Lydia could be.

"My dear Lydia," Mrs. Bennet began, after situating herself close to her youngest daughter in the drawing room. "How happy you must be to see your dear husband regaining his childhood friend."

"I do not know what you mean," Lydia replied.

"Why, Mr. Darcy of course. Dear Wickham must be so pleased that his old friend has shown such an interest in his marriage to actually come and visit your family. It is too bad that you will be sent away to the North so soon and they will not be able to continue to be in each other's company."

"Oh, we will not miss the likes of Mr. Darcy," Lydia replied with a laugh. "He always stands there so solemnly and never says anything; so different from my own husband. Dear George was very surprised when Mr. Darcy arrived here the day after we did.

We were both quite sure that after our wedding we would never see him again."

"Do you mean to say he was at the wedding?" Mrs. Bennet asked.

Elizabeth, fearing (rightly) that Lydia was about to share information that she had promised to keep secret, tried to distract her mother by asking Lydia about the type of lace on her wedding gown. Although this would normally have been a good tactic, Mrs. Bennet was a woman on a mission. She interrupted Lydia's description of the lace (it was the third time since arriving that she had described it) and asked again about the presence of Mr. Darcy at the wedding.

"Well, yes," Lydia replied, "for someone had to stand up with Wickham and none of the officers could be spared. Oh, how I wish he could have been married in his red coat."

"Mr. Darcy stood up with Mr. Wickham?" Mrs. Bennet asked excitedly. It was better than she had hoped. If Mr. Darcy and Mr. Wickham were on such terms that Mr. Darcy could stand up for Mr. Wickham at his wedding, then surely they were only a few nudges away from having Mr. Darcy offer a living to Mr. Wickham. Surely, kind, affable Mr. Wickham did not want to hinder the regrowth of his friendship with unhappy memories. Mr. Darcy just needed to be reminded that if he offered a living to Mr. Wickham they could regularly be in each other's company and could overcome any misunderstandings from the past.

With Mrs. Bennet left to her musings (a rare occurrence in the presence of others), Elizabeth was able to steer Lydia far away from the topic of her wedding, in hopes that she could avoid any further mention of Mr. Darcy's involvement. Her mother may not have caught the significance of Mr. Darcy being at the wedding, but Mr. Darcy still wanted his involvement to be kept a secret, and she would do her best to honor his wishes.

When the gentlemen rejoined the ladies, Fitzwilliam Darcy immediately sought out his beloved. Knowing the hour of separation was coming to a close, Elizabeth had separated herself from her mother and sisters, finding an unobtrusive position along the edges of the room, next to a window. Feigning an interest in the view from the window, Darcy moved to Elizabeth's side.

"What is troubling you?" he quietly queried. It was clear from the look on Elizabeth's face that something was on her mind.

"Lydia," was her one word reply.

"You may not envy her position, but she made her own decisions. She is not concerned about the man she has married. She will undoubtedly discover his true disposition soon enough. Try not to ruin the short time of marital bliss that she is currently enjoying."

"That is not what I was thinking about," Elizabeth replied, with a scowl. "I will have plenty of time to feel sorry for her when she finally realizes she has made a mistake."

"Then what is worrying you?"

"She told my mother you were at her wedding."

"I will never understand how the two of you could possibly be related."

Unknown to the participants in this discussion, Darcy and Elizabeth were being observed by both Mr. and Mrs. Bennet, but for two very different reasons. Mr. Bennet was delighted at the appearance of the scowl on his daughter's face, so quickly followed by a look of annoyance from Mr. Darcy before his mask was back in place. He would find some time in the morning to talk with his favorite daughter so that he could find

out what sort of disagreement they had, and encourage her to
send Mr. Darcy away.

Mrs. Bennet, on the other hand, was concerned that Elizabeth
might be scaring away Mr. Darcy. If her outspoken daughter
scared Mr. Darcy away before he could offer a living to Mr.
Wickham, then all would be lost. Wickham and Lydia would
leave for Newcastle, possibly to never see Mr. Darcy again. She
could not let that happen. She had to intervene. She moved
across the room. It was time to stem the tide of Elizabeth's
tongue.

Elizabeth was confused.

Mrs. Bennet had purposefully made her way across the room to
sit next to Elizabeth. She had then begun an obnoxious flattery of
Mr. Darcy, not letting either of them get a word in edgewise.
Mrs. Bennet had never spoken a civil word toward Mr. Darcy (or
even about Mr. Darcy), so Elizabeth was confused as to why her
sudden change of heart. She could only sit back and let her
mother rattle on, casting an apologetic look in Mr. Darcy's
direction.

After complimenting Mr. Darcy on his taste in clothes, carriages,
home (though she had never seen it), and anything else she could
think of, Mrs. Bennet finally came to her point.

"You must be delighted to see your old friend so happily
married," Mrs. Bennet said. Mr. Darcy nodded his ascent, though
it took him a while to realize she was referring to Mr. Wickham.
"How unfortunate that the newlyweds must go as far away as
Newcastle. If only there was a living that was available closer to
home, then you would be able to see your old friend so much
more often."

"Indeed," was Mr. Darcy's only reply, but it was encouragement
enough for Mrs. Bennet.

"With an estate as vast as yours, I am sure you are always looking for someone to fill some sort of living or another," Mrs. Bennet continued. "If you had Mr. Wickham fill one of those livings you would have the peace of mind knowing such a dear old friend was so well taken care of, and that the living would be so well watched over."

Mr. Darcy was stunned. He couldn't even manage a grunt or a nod. This woman was impossible. He glanced at Elizabeth, wondering again how she could have possibly been raised by such a woman.

Elizabeth, on the other hand, had had enough. Her mother had gone too far.

"You cannot possibly be suggesting that Mr. Darcy should offer Mr. Wickham a living in the church," Elizabeth exclaimed. "He could not possibly be fit for such a position."

"And why not," Mrs. Bennet replied. "They have been friends since childhood, and now that Mr. Wickham is so happily married to Lydia, I do not see that there can be any impediments."

Suddenly aware of the presence of others in the room (it was a dinner party), Elizabeth leaned toward her mother, so she could speak with little chance of being overheard.

"You know perfectly well why Mr. Wickham is not fit for the church," she whispered. "You will not bring this up again."

"Ungrateful child," Mrs. Bennet whispered back. "You will not speak to me in this manner. Just because you did not see fit to marry a clergyman in order to provide for the security of our family does not mean that you should step in the way of a secure living for Mr. Wickham. He will take care of us when Mr. Collins is ready to throw us into the hedgerows."

"I sincerely doubt that Charlotte will encourage Mr. Collins to throw us into the hedgerows," Elizabeth replied, happy that her mother had switched to another one of her favorite topics.

"But we cannot be sure," she replied. "If you had only agreed to marry the man, then I am sure we would all be safe. There is no way Mr. Collins would abandon his own wife's family when he inherits. Now, I am sure he is so upset with us because of your refusal that we will be cast into the hedgerows while your father is still warm in his grave."

Mr. Darcy had turned pale. Mr. Collins had actually asked Elizabeth to marry him, and from the sounds of it her mother had tried desperately to get Elizabeth to accept him. If Elizabeth had been willing to marry for material reasons, then when he saw her again at Rosings it would have been as Mr. Collins' wife instead of his wife's friend. He was suddenly very grateful that Elizabeth's principles would not allow her to marry a man that she did not love.

As the dinner party ended, the Bennet family rose to see their guests to their carriages. Having positioned himself on the far side of the room, Darcy was easily able to position himself to be the last of the visitors to depart. As Mrs. Bennet bounded her way to the front of the party in order to personally wish each guest safe travels (and gloat once more that she had a daughter married), Mr. Darcy took the opportunity to speak quietly with Elizabeth.

"I did not realize how closely I came to losing you."

"At the time, I was not yours to lose," Elizabeth replied.

"Yes, but I did not know that," Mr. Darcy said. "If you remember, I was so conceited that I thought you were anticipating my addresses. If I had courted you properly from the beginning, Mr. Collins would have never offered for you. If only

I had learned my lesson earlier. We could have been married by now."

"It will not be long, my love," Elizabeth replied quietly. "In a few months we will be able to look back and laugh at our impatience."

"I sincerely hope so," Mr. Darcy replied, bringing Elizabeth's hand to his lips for a lingering kiss. "Right now all I can think of is marrying you and taking you home. I cannot wait to bring you back to Pemberley, this time as my wife."

Thinking they had miraculously been left alone for a minute, Mr. Darcy almost leaned in for a quick kiss, until he saw a slight movement out of the corner of his eye and turned to see Mary sitting close by, looking at them with wide eyes. Embarrassed, Darcy gave a slight nod in her direction, gave a quick farewell to Elizabeth, then left the drawing room to join the rest of the party goers waiting for their conveyance home.

Mary found herself wishing again that she was not so invisible. It was clear that her sister and Mr. Darcy were not aware of her presence in the room. During their foray into the garden the day before, Mary had realized that her sister had drastically changed her opinion concerning Mr. Darcy. She knew Mr. Darcy had only cut a bouquet for her because he was cutting one for Elizabeth. As she overheard their conversation, she realized that they needed to be alerted to her presence. She very deliberately waved her book in the air as she set it on the table to her side.

After Mr. Darcy left the room, Elizabeth came to sit on the settee next to Mary.

"I'm sorry if we made you uncomfortable," Elizabeth started, a little flushed. "I'm afraid to admit we were so unaware of our surroundings that I did not see you."

"You do not need to apologize for not seeing me," Mary replied. "I know that I often blend in to the background."

"Do not think that," Elizabeth replied, guiltily. "If I had not been so preoccupied I would have known you were there."

"You did seem to have a lot to discuss with Mr. Darcy."

"Mary, how much did you overhear?" Elizabeth asked.

"Enough to know you are secretly engaged," Mary admitted. "You must know that I cannot condone a secret engagement. I do not even understand the reason for it. Why has he not approached Papa?"

"He has approached Papa," Elizabeth said. "Papa has refused his consent."

"But why?" Mary asked, surprised.

"That is none of your concern." The displeased voice of Mr. Bennet surprised both girls, and they jumped simultaneously. They had not realized their father had returned to the drawing room.

Gathering her courage, Mary resolved to do something she had never done before: Openly question one of her father's decisions.

"Mr. Darcy is a good man. Why would you not allow Lizzy to marry him when it would obviously make her happy to become his wife?"

"There are things you do not understand," Mr. Bennet replied, coldly. "Nor will I be explaining them to you."

Mr. Bennet's tone of voice made it clear the discussion was over. Quietly, Mary and Elizabeth excused themselves to prepare for bed. As they parted ways at Elizabeth's door, Mary gathered her elder sister into her arms.

"If you ever want to talk about it, know I am available," Mary whispered. "I am really good at sitting quietly and listening."

With a laugh, Elizabeth thanked her sister for the offer. She did not want to burden Jane with any troubles beyond her own. If things became worse, then maybe she could unload her troubles on her sister, Mary, instead.

Chapter 8

Elizabeth was starting to appreciate her sister Mary. As Elizabeth prepared for her morning walk, Mary joined her. Mary was habitually an early riser, but typically used the quiet of the morning for personal spiritual reflection and doctrinal study. Although she was loath to skip her daily studies, she recognized that her sister needed her. Vowing not to make a habit of it, Mary donned her outerwear.

Although their walk commenced in silence, the silence did not long remain. Mary had accurately described herself when she had told her sister that she was good at sitting (or in this case walking) quietly and listening. Elizabeth's mind had been in such turmoil that it was not long before she was telling her sister everything (well, almost everything, she still wasn't ready to tell anyone but Jane about Mr. Darcy's letter).

"I still do not understand why Papa will not give his consent," Mary said. "It is clear you have come to care about Mr. Darcy."

"Papa seems to think the only reason I want to marry Mr. Darcy is to avoid a scandal. After the mess with Lydia he is not inclined to pressure any of us to marry over something as simple as a kiss."

Mary did not feel a kiss was a simple thing, but had to admit to herself that it was definitely a lot different from what Lydia had done.

"Surely now that he has seen the two of you together, he must realize how much you care for each other," Mary said. "When was the last time you talked to him about Mr. Darcy?"

"It was before Fitzwilliam asked him for my hand," Elizabeth confessed. "I'm afraid I was quite distraught when he told me he was going to refuse him. I haven't been able to talk to him since."

"When was that?"

"The day after we received the letter from Uncle Gardiner letting us know that Lydia had been found."

Every member of the Bennet family was aware of the close relationship between Elizabeth and Mr. Bennet. Mary was astounded to hear that Elizabeth had not had a conversation with their father for more than a week.

"He does seem aware that you and Mr. Darcy still plan to be wed," Mary indicated.

"Yes, when Fitzwilliam talked to him he refused his consent, but indicated that if he would take up residence in the area, and we still wanted to marry after I come of age, that he will give me his blessing. He has made it very clear, though, that in the mean time we should not consider ourselves engaged."

"There are less than two months now before you come of age. That is not too long of a time."

"I keep telling myself that, but it still breaks my heart knowing that Papa wants me to change my mind. He wants me to break the unofficial engagement and send Fitzwilliam away."

"It has been over a week since you talked to him. Maybe you should try again."

Elizabeth looked at her sister, wondering what happened to the meek young lady that never gave advice that didn't come first from Fordyce. With these thoughts in her head, she couldn't help but smile at Mary's next words.

"In his sermons, Fordyce admonishes us to give up our pride and stubbornness. If you lay aside your pride and talk to Papa, maybe he will be able to lay aside his stubbornness and listen to you."

As Elizabeth and Mary returned to the house from their morning walk, Elizabeth decided to seek out her father in his study. She was afraid that if she waited any longer her courage would fail her.

"Could I talk to you Papa," Elizabeth asked quietly, opening the door to find her father sitting in one of his chairs, looking absently out the window. He looked tired and worn, as if he had aged a decade over the course of the previous month.

Mr. Bennet looked at his daughter silently for a few minutes before replying.

"What can I do for you, Lizzy?" he asked.

"I have missed our conversations," she replied. "It wasn't until I was talking to Mary this morning that I realized how long it has been since I joined you in your study."

"Or had a pleasant conversation," he replied. After a few more minutes of observing his daughter he continued. "I want to do what is best for you, my dear."

"I know that," she replied. "You have always tried to give me what I need." After a few more minutes, she added, quietly: "Can you not see that I need to marry Mr. Darcy?"

"Why? Why do you need to marry him?"

"Because I love him. I will never love anyone else the way that I love him."

After studying his daughter quietly for a few more minutes, he whispered a quiet, "I see," then invited her to a game of chess.

They were still sitting across the chess board, having ignored their breakfast, when Mr. Darcy arrived a few hours later.

Fitzwilliam Darcy was surprised to see Elizabeth sitting across a chess board from her father when he was shown into the study. After a quiet greeting to both, he took the offered seat close to Elizabeth.

"Would you mind telling me how you came to be at my daughter's wedding?" Mr. Bennet asked quietly, after moving one of his chess pieces.

Darcy glanced at Elizabeth, who gave a very subtle shake of her head to indicate that she had not said anything.

"I am sorry, exceedingly sorry," replied Darcy, in a tone of surprise and emotion, "that you have ever been informed of what may, in a mistaken light, have given you uneasiness. May I enquire how you have come to know of my involvement?"

"Last night my wife told me of your presence as proof that you still consider Mr. Wickham a dear friend, and encouraged me to try to persuade you to provide him a living. Since I know that is not true, I became very curious as to the real reason for your presence."

Darcy gazed at Elizabeth, trying to determine the best way to proceed. With a slight smile from her, he answered.

"I came upon Miss Elizabeth shortly after she received her letters from Miss Bennet," Darcy explained. "It was clear that she was upset. When she explained what had happened to cause her distress, I determined to do all within my power to bring her relief. It was my responsibility."

"Why did you consider it your responsibility?"

"For two reasons. First, I love your daughter. I consider myself promised to her. I would do anything in my power to make her happy." After a slight pause, Darcy continued. "Second, as you are aware, I have known Mr. Wickham all my life. I am aware of his tendencies. If I had warned you properly this could not have happened. It was my responsibility."

"When I left London, my brother Gardiner and I had only met dead ends," Mr. Bennet said. "When I received the express indicating that they had been found, I was too relieved to question how he had gone from a dead end to having a negotiated marriage within only a couple of days. It would appear I owe you for the marriage of my youngest daughter."

"You owe me nothing, sir," Darcy replied.

"Yet, it appears as if you are going to take my Lizzy, anyway."

"And do I now have your permission to do so?" Darcy asked after a slight pause.

"Yes, I suppose that is the only thing that I can give you as payment for saving our family from ridicule and scorn."

"Truly, Papa?" Elizabeth asked.

"Truly, my dear," Mr. Bennet replied. "Now, I am going to give you five minutes on your own. I feel I owe you something." Abandoning the chess game, Mr. Bennet stood and walked out of the room, leaving Elizabeth and Darcy alone for the first time since she had agreed to marry him.

Both Elizabeth and Darcy had risen as Mr. Bennet left the room. They stared at each other for a full thirty seconds before Darcy raised his hand to stroke Elizabeth's face. After running his fingers the length of her jaw, he cupped her face in the palm of his hand and leaned close.

"I will always love you, Elizabeth," he whispered.

"I will always love you, Fitzwilliam," she replied.

Elizabeth reached on her tiptoes to close the gap between their lips. They were thus engaged when Mrs. Bennet came rushing through the door moments later.

When Elizabeth had confessed her love for Mr. Darcy, Mr. Bennet knew that it was time to grant his consent. When he had read the postscript to the express telling him that Mr. Darcy had kissed his daughter, Elizabeth, and would be arriving soon to ask for her hand in marriage, he was not ready to be pressured into granting that request. He had not been ready see that they were in love.

He still did not know how it had happened, but it was clear that it had. Elizabeth had fallen in love.

As he left the study, he caught sight of his wife descending the stairs. He decided that if he was going to have to give up his daughter, he should at least get some entertainment from it.

"Mrs. Bennet," he called. "If you are inclined to pay a visit to my study you will find one of your daughters with her betrothed. I am sure she will want to introduce you."

"How you tease me," Mrs. Bennet replied. "You know that none of my daughters have been entertaining suitors recently."

"Well, if you can think of another reason Mr. Darcy would be requesting a private audience with one of our daughters, I would like to hear it."

"Truly, Mr. Bennet?"

"Truly, my dear."

Even though Darcy and Elizabeth were engaged in a passionate embrace when Mrs. Bennet opened the door to the study, she rushed toward them to offer her congratulations and well wishes as profusely as possible. She grabbed each of them by the arm, to bring them to the drawing room so they could announce their happy news to the rest of the family.

Kitty and Lydia were the only members of the household that were actually surprised by the news, though both Jane and Mary were surprised that their father had granted his permission when he had sworn he would not.

It was not long before Lydia went from happily surprised for her sister, to incredibly unhappy. As her mother rattled on about how grand the wedding would be, how much pin money Elizabeth would have, and how the other girls would now be thrown into the paths of other rich men, Lydia became down right incensed. She had delighted in being married before any of her sisters. It had been a point of great pride to be able to walk in front of all her sisters while entering the home or going into dinner. She had expected to be able to lord it over her sisters for years to come. Now, Elizabeth was getting married to someone of much greater consequence. She would not be able to hold her new position of highest ranking sister for any length of time. *It was not fair.*

When Wickham finally arose from his bed and joined the family party, Lydia tried to steer the conversation back to his heroic actions the evening before that had earned him a broken nose after getting kicked in the face by his horse. Wickham was more than happy to oblige, and even Mr. Darcy seemed to encourage him to tell his tale. Lydia thought it was the worst type of betrayal when Kitty asked their mother if she could get a new gown for the wedding. That turned the conversation to lace, and what would be required in a wedding gown for such a lady as Elizabeth would now be.

With a huff, Lydia grabbed the arm of her husband and they set out on a walk. She would have been crushed to realize that her mother was hardly even aware of her leaving.

Chapter 9

Fitzwilliam Darcy was pleased that his engagement to Elizabeth Bennet was now official, but disappointed that his wedding date had not changed. When Mr. Bennet had given his consent a little over a week previous, Darcy had hoped to move up his wedding date by several weeks. He did not take into account his future mother-in-law. It now became clear that if things had gone according to the original plan she would have been quite put out by having a mere month to plan the wedding of her second child. The wedding was still set for one month after Elizabeth's birthday. With her birthday still a month away, Mr. Darcy was trying his best to wait patiently.

Mrs. Bennet had felt cheated when she was unable to plan Lydia's wedding. Although she bragged as much as possible about the fact that she had a daughter married, she knew their neighbors were not completely ignorant of the circumstances surrounding Lydia's marriage (as much as she liked to pretend otherwise). Now that Elizabeth was marrying Mr. Darcy, she could not believe her good luck. It would probably be best not to speculate on how many seconds it took for Elizabeth to rise in status from the least favorite child *(How could she have jeopardized the future of the family by refusing to marry Mr. Collins?)* to most favorite child *(Oh, what jewels she will have! What pin money! 10,000 a year! She will save us all!)*.

Mrs. Bennet was now in the midst of planning the grandest wedding that Meryton Society had ever witnessed. Although Elizabeth knew that her tastes did not always coincide with that of her mother's, she was also aware that by allowing her mother to have her way with the wedding preparations, she would have more time available to spend with Mr. Darcy. The only item that Elizabeth was adamant about having her own way was the wedding gown. Mrs. Bennet had long ago realized that her daughter could not be convinced to the proper amount of lace to trim her gowns, and had been happy to reach this compromise with Elizabeth as well. Elizabeth would choose her own gown. Mrs. Bennet would choose everything else.

Through this time Lydia became more and more agitated. For the first few days after Elizabeth and Darcy announced their engagement she had continued to accompany her mother on her visits with the neighbors. As the rest of the neighborhood also showed very little interest in Lydia and Wickham now that Elizabeth was engaged to a man worth 10,000 a year, she quickly tired of these visits as well.

The Wickhams' visit was coming to an end, and no one was happier about this than Lydia. The final straw had come when all the Bennet girls were preparing to go to town to be measured for new gowns for the wedding. Lydia was in her room preparing herself as well, assuming she would be included, even though she would be in Newcastle before the wedding, and as a married woman her parents would no longer be responsible for her expenses. She had never been denied a treat before, and did not imagine that Wickham would deny her this.

"Where are you going?" Wickham asked her.

"Momma is taking all the girls to town to be measured for gowns for the wedding."

"We will be gone long before the wedding, there is no need for you to get a new gown," he replied.

"But everyone else will be receiving new gowns, I should like one as well," Lydia said with a pout.

"Well, if you can convince your mother to buy you a new gown you are welcome, but you will not be buying a new gown. You had several new gowns made up before we were married."

"But that was before going to Brighton."

Although Lydia continued to entreat her husband, he would not be moved. Eventually, she decided to try her luck with her mother. Her mother was also deaf to Lydia's entreaties. No matter what Lydia said, Mrs. Bennet would not agree to buy her a new dress. Finally, Mrs. Bennet admitted that Mr. Bennet had made it clear that she was not to shower Lydia with any presents before leaving or she would find herself unable to spend as much on Elizabeth's wedding as she would hope. Previously, this would not have stopped Mrs. Bennet, but she was much more interested in showing her superiority to her neighbors than she was in indulging her youngest daughter.

With tears in her eyes, Lydia turned toward Elizabeth as she made her way down the stairs. "Why could you not wait until I was gone to become engaged," she cried. "You are so selfish. I hate you, Lizzy!"

With this pronouncement, Lydia ran from the house. Elizabeth encouraged her mother and sisters to go on to Meryton without her, then followed Lydia into the garden.

It took a few minutes for Elizabeth to find Lydia, but eventually she was drawn by the sound of her sobs to a secluded bench in the rear of the gardens.

"What are you doing here?" Lydia asked. "Why are you not on your way to Meryton?"

"I can go to the dressmaker's later," Elizabeth replied. "I thought we should talk."

"There is nothing you can say that I want to hear."

They sat in silence for a few minutes. Lydia broke it before Elizabeth.

"Well, don't you have a lecture for me?" Lydia asked.

"I didn't come to lecture you. I came to tell you a story."

Although Lydia did not want to admit it, her curiosity was getting the better of her.

"What type of story?"

"A love story," Elizabeth replied.

"Well, get on with it then," Lydia said when Elizabeth did not elaborate.

"Once upon a time there was a gentleman and a young lady who loved each other very much, though they had tried very hard to hide their feelings. While the young lady was on holiday with her aunt and uncle she happened to meet the gentleman while touring his estate. As soon as they saw each other they realized they could not deny their feelings for each other, so they became engaged. Before the gentleman had the opportunity to travel to the young lady's home and ask her father for her hand, the young lady got some distressing news from home. Her youngest sister had eloped."

"So, you were already engaged before I was married?" Lydia interrupted.

"I do not believe I mentioned the name of the gentleman and the young lady," Elizabeth replied. "Now, where was I? Oh yes. The young lady was very upset because she was extremely worried about her youngest sister. According to the reports, her sister and her lover had only been traced to London. There was no sign of them on any of the roads to Scotland."

"We were only delayed by business for a few days," Lydia interrupted again. "We would have travelled on to Scotland eventually. Wickham promised we would be married."

"As I was saying," Elizabeth continued, "The gentleman volunteered to go to London to help discover his beloved's younger sister. Once there, he did everything he could to help the young couple get married as quickly as possible, he even arranged for all of the other gentleman's debts to be paid so that the married couple could start life with a clean slate."

"Why would he do that?"

"He never gave an explanation, but I like to think it is because he loved his betrothed very much, and would do anything in his power to make her happy."

At some point during the narration Lydia found herself leaning up against her sister. Elizabeth pulled her up against her shoulder.

"Why did it take so long for you to announce your engagement?"

"You may remember that when Mr. Darcy was visiting Mr. Bingley last year he did not make a good impression on Meryton society. Papa did not believe that I loved him. Initially, he refused his consent."

"Why did he change his mind?" Lydia asked.

"He came to see how much Mr. Darcy and I have come to love each other," Elizabeth replied.

"Why could you not at least have waited until after I left to announce your engagement? Now, no one cares that I am the first one married. No one cares about me at all."

"Never think that," Elizabeth replied. "We all care about you very much. You are my sister. You may aggravate me at times, but I will always love you."

One would hope that this conversation would have a lasting change on Lydia. Unfortunately, she was still a 15 year old girl that had spent the better part of her life getting everything that she wanted. She was no longer upset with the engagement of Elizabeth and Mr. Darcy, but in all other parts of her life, she was much as she ever was.

Upon returning to the house before leaving for Meryton, Elizabeth was surprised to find Jane waiting for her. After putting on their bonnets and spencers they set out on their way to Meryton.

"How is Lydia doing?" Jane asked.

"She has calmed down," Elizabeth replied.

They walked in silence for some time. This time, it was Elizabeth that broke the silence.

"How are you doing, Jane?" she asked.

"I will be well," she replied. "At least now I know why Mr. Bingley left. He must have realized how much I had come to care for him, and left so that it would not be awkward between us. Now that I know, I will be able to forget about him."

"You are too, too good, Jane."

"I do have one favor to ask," Jane said. "When he brings his bride to Netherfield, may I come and stay with you? He should be able to introduce his wife to Meryton society without me there."

"We will be happy to have you visit us anytime that you desire," Elizabeth replied. "But do not let him make you feel uncomfortable in your own home. You have nothing to be ashamed of."

It is difficult to determine who was more relieved when the day came for the Wickhams to leave Longbourn and travel to Newcastle.

Lydia was relieved as she would no longer be losing in the competition for her mother's attention with her sister Elizabeth.

Wickham was relieved as he would no longer be subject to the cold glares directed at him by Mr. Darcy.

Kitty was relieved as Lydia would no longer be boasting about the fact that she was the first to marry.

Mary was relieved as she really had never forgiven Lydia and Wickham for eloping (though she really was trying, and forgiveness would come, but not right then).

Mr. Bennet was relieved as he would no longer have to pretend to his neighbors that he felt no ill will towards any members of his household.

Mrs. Bennet was relieved as she would not have to keep thwarting Lydia's requests for new clothes and trinkets (she really did want to give these things to Lydia, and it broke her heart to have to deny Lydia anything).

Mr. Darcy was relieved as he really could not stand the sight of Mr. Wickham (and he could now invite Georgiana to come and visit).

Elizabeth was relieved as she also could not stand the sight of Mr. Wickham (and the thought that Mr. and Mrs. Wickham were now sharing Lydia's childhood bed chamber turned her stomach).

Jane was relieved because everyone else was relieved, and the release of tension was a palatable thing.

The day after the Wickhams departed, all the females in the Bennet household could be found scouring the society pages in the newspaper. The engagement announcement had been sent, and should be run today. Mrs. Bennet was the first to find it, and read it excitedly to the rest of the room.

After the excitement had died down, Elizabeth claimed the newspaper so she could cut out the announcement to include in her journal. As she scanned the rest of the page, her eyes were arrested by one of the announcements. She surreptitiously cut that one out as well, secreting it in her dress pocket.

Elizabeth and Darcy were enjoying an afternoon stroll in the garden (chaperoned by Mary, who was reading from Fordyce's Sermons). They had started most properly with Elizabeth's hand on Darcy's elbow. Before long, they had switched to the slightly less proper hand holding.

"Did you see that our engagement announcement was in the newspaper today, Fitzwilliam?" Elizabeth queried.

"I must admit I did not look at the society pages before leaving Netherfield, I was much more anxious to arrive at Longbourn,"

Darcy replied, using his thumb to stroke the back of her hand. "Was it put in properly?"

"Yes, of course," Elizabeth replied. "Though, I must admit I was intrigued by another announcement that was also published this morning."

"Anyone that I know?" Darcy asked, bringing her hand to his mouth for a kiss.

"Yes, I believe you know the parties involved, but I must admit that I have never met the happy couple."

"It was not Bingley's announcement then? It has now been a year since they became engaged, so the announcement should be published soon."

"That is what I found intriguing," Elizabeth admitted. "The announcement was for a Miss Georgiana Crawford, but the gentleman was not Mr. Bingley."

"Are you sure?" Darcy asked, confused. "I would have thought Bingley would have told me if his engagement had been broken."

Elizabeth pulled the announcement out of her pocket and handed it to Mr. Darcy. The announcement did indeed indicate that Miss Georgiana Crawford was engaged to be married, but, instead of Mr. Bingley, the groom was the Viscount Timothy Rawlings.

Chapter 10

Fitzwilliam Darcy was content. His engagement to Elizabeth had been acknowledged. The Wickhams had left, so he was now free to invite Georgiana to stay with him (though it would be a couple of days before she would arrive). And his engagement announcement had been published in the newspaper, so it was unlikely that Mr. Bennet would rescind his permission.

He was still confused at the engagement announcement for Miss Crawford, and had sent a letter to Bingley after returning to Netherfield the day before. He expected it would be at least a day or two before he received an answer, though, as Mr. Bingley was not known for his diligence in correspondence.

As he was preparing for his daily visit to Longbourn, he was surprised to hear the arrival of a carriage. His glance out the window revealed none other than Mr. Bingley. Darcy was not prepared for the joy that infused his friend's face as he joined him in the library.

"You must congratulate me, Darcy, I am the happiest of men!" Bingley announced as he entered the room.

"What has made you so happy?" Darcy asked. He knew Bingley could not have had a chance to visit Longbourn.

"Miss Crawford has thrown me over!" he replied.

"I find myself confused," Darcy admitted. "Perhaps you should tell me the story from the beginning."

"Well, about a week after you left us at Pemberley, we made our way back to London. We had come to visit you, not your home. Well, at least that was my intent, though Caroline kept making such pointed references concerning your sister and myself, that it became uncomfortable for the both of us. Retreat seemed the best option.

"After returning to London, I paid an unexpected call to Miss Crawford. They had not been expecting me in town for a couple more weeks. When I arrived, I was surprised to find Miss Crawford in a relatively private conversation with Viscount Rawlings. From her blush, it was clear she was enjoying the conversation.

"That day, I did not have an opportunity to talk to her privately, but determined to call the next day. We had been engaged for almost a year, but I had seen very little of her during that time, due to the request of her father.

"The next day, I returned to the Crawford home, with hopes to speak to Miss Crawford. My intents were thwarted again, as well as the next day. I was beginning to become suspicious, so I requested a private audience with her father. Mr. Crawford admitted that his daughter was becoming attached to Viscount Rawlings. Since we had agreed to a year before announcing the engagement, it would appear he felt that he could use that time to encourage his daughter to loftier ambitions."

"But, you were engaged!" Darcy interrupted.

"Yes, and if I felt any more than a passing fancy for Miss Crawford, I would no doubt now be enraged," Bingley replied. "As it is, I can only find relief. As it turns out, Viscount Rawlings had taken the time to solicit Miss Crawford's hand in marriage while I was talking to her father. He was waiting outside his study when I emerged, requesting consent to the engagement."

"But, they have used you most abominably," Darcy said. "Did David know of this?" David Crawford had been a friend to both Darcy and Bingley while at Cambridge. The idea that he would be party to this duplicity was unbelievable.

"No, David had no idea. He has been much engaged at managing their estate in Dorset. His father has already passed on most of those responsibilities, allowing Mr. Crawford to spend more time in town. David had recently returned to London as well, so when I wished Miss Crawford a very cool farewell, he followed me out.

"We went to White's together, where I told him my story. I have to admit that even then I was beginning to feel a little high-spirited, thinking that now I was free to return to Netherfield and resume my addresses to my Angel. David was relieved I was not upset, and would not let the actions of the rest of his family ruin our friendship. It was clear he did not want to speak too harshly against his sister, but he did go so far as to say his cousin Henry would likely be proud of her."

"That's not much of a compliment," Darcy replied with a laugh.

"No, I do not think it was meant as a compliment, but rather as a way to show his feelings about the situation without making a scene at the club. We parted amicably, then I returned to my townhouse to prepare to come to Hertfordshire. It was a few days before my business could be satisfactorily concluded so that I would not be distracted when I arrived."

"So, you have returned to Netherfield, intent on winning the hand of Miss Bennet?" Darcy asked.

"Yes, she is the dearest creature I have ever known. I have long regretted my hasty engagement to Miss Crawford, and can only thank the hand of providence that has allowed me another chance to win her hand. I know that you did not feel she had any tender feelings for me, and with that in mind I could not feel proper motivation to break my engagement. Now that I am free I will do all in my power to engage her feelings."

"I must admit something to you, Bingley," Darcy replied. "After we left Netherfield last fall, Jane went to London. While there she visited with your sister, and Caroline returned her visit as well. In addition, as recently as last April, Elizabeth assured me that her sister was in love with you. I did not share this with you because I did not think it would be appropriate. You were engaged to another woman. At the time, I could only feel that this knowledge would give you unwanted pain."

"Yes, of course you were right," Bingley replied. "But, can you not see how wonderful that makes things now! If she has cared for me, then it surely will not take long for me to reignite those feelings. Now, when are you going to Longbourn to visit your lovely Miss Elizabeth?"

"I was just getting ready to leave when you arrived," Darcy replied with a laugh. "Do you care to refresh yourself before we leave, or were you planning on arriving at Longbourn in your travelling clothes, with the fresh dirt from the road still clinging to you?"

"Yes, of course," Bingley replied. "Give me ten minutes and I'll be ready." With that, he nearly ran from the room, ascending the stairs while calling for his valet.

Elizabeth was sitting in the drawing room with her mother and her sisters, wondering why Darcy was later than usual this morning, when she heard the approach of a carriage. *That's odd,* she thought, *he always comes on horseback.*

Her musings were short lived, when she heard a very strident voice in the hall. At first, she could not believe she recognized the voice correctly. Quickly, though, the door was thrown wide open and their visitor entered. It was Lady Catherine de Bourgh.

She entered the room with an air more than usually ungracious, made no other reply to Elizabeth's salutation than a slight inclination of the head, and sat down without saying a word. Elizabeth had mentioned her name to her mother on her ladyship's entrance, though no request of introduction had been made.

It was not long before Elizabeth realized she was in effect participating in a staring match with Darcy's Aunt Catherine. Evidently, she won, as after a few minutes Lady Catherine demanded that Elizabeth attend her in the prettyish kind of a little wilderness on the side of their lawn.

As soon as they entered the copse, Lady Catherine began in the following manner: "You can be at no loss, Miss Bennet, to understand the reason of my journey hither. Your own heart, your own conscience, must tell you why I come."

"I can only imagine that you have come to congratulate me on my engagement to your nephew," Elizabeth replied. "The announcement was run just yesterday, so I find myself flattered at your hasty journey to congratulate us."

"Obstinate, headstrong girl. You must know I have not come to offer my congratulations, but to put a stop to this absurdity. This match, to which you have the presumption to aspire, can never take place. No, never. Mr. Darcy is engaged to my daughter."

"Mr. Darcy is a gentleman of the highest order. You would do better than to slander his name by claiming an engagement where there is none. He would never have made an offer to me if he was so engaged."

"The engagement between them is of a peculiar kind. From their infancy, they have been intended for each other. It was the favorite wish of his mother, as well as of hers. While in their cradles, we planned the union: and now, at the moment when the wishes of both sisters would be accomplished in their marriage, to be prevented by a young woman of inferior birth, of no importance in the world, and wholly unallied to the family!"

"But what is that to me? If there is no other objection to my marrying your nephew, I shall certainly not be kept from it by knowing that his mother and aunt wished him to marry Miss de Bourgh. You both did as much as you could in planning the marriage. Its completion depended on others. If Mr. Darcy is neither by honor nor inclination confined to his cousin, why is not he to make another choice? And as I am that choice, I see no reason why I should not accept him. In any event, I find your objections are ill timed. The announcement has been run in the newspapers. To break it off now would cause a scandal."

"Do not think I have not considered this, Miss Bennet," Lady Catherine replied angrily. "I had received a letter from Mr. Darcy telling me of his engagement a couple of days ago, and immediately set out to put this to rights. I made it as far as London yesterday. When I arrived, I saw the announcement in the newspaper. I have spent all my time since that moment devising stratagems to avoid this catastrophe."

"I am sorry that you have wasted your most diligent efforts," Elizabeth said. "There has not been a catastrophe. You will not need to utilize any of the stratagems you have concocted."

"I will not be interrupted!" Lady Catherine bellowed. "You will listen to me, and do as I say. Now, I am not unaware that Mrs. Collins has two brothers that are as yet unmarried. I will allow you your choice between the two of them. We will send a correction to the newspaper, announcing Darcy's marriage to Anne and your engagement to whichever Mr. Lucas you prefer. It will run with an apology from the newspaper for the mix-up, stating that the two announcements were somehow combined."

"You cannot possibly be serious," Elizabeth replied. "Even you must realize you do not have the power to control people's lives in this way. What makes you think that either Mr. Darcy or I would agree to this subterfuge? What about the Lucas's? Neither of them have ever shown a preference for me, and I doubt they can be commanded into feeling affection for their sister's friend, when we have known each other all our lives and it has not grown naturally."

"You are to understand, Miss Bennet, that I came here with the determined resolution of carrying my purpose; nor will I be dissuaded from it. I have not been used to submit to any person's whims. I have not been in the habit of brooking disappointment."

"That will make your ladyship's situation at present more pitiable; but it will have no effect on me."

Any future comment by Lady Catherine was prevented by the arrival of Mr. Darcy. Darcy and Bingley had arrived at Netherfield only a few minutes previous. When Darcy had discerned that it was his aunt's carriage standing in front of Longbourn, he nearly ran inside. He was relieved that Lady Catherine was not in the drawing room with the rest of the Bennet ladies, but since there was also no sign of Elizabeth he remained agitated.

Mrs. Bennet had just begun her effusive welcome of Mr. Bingley, when Mr. Darcy interrupted her, asking where Elizabeth and his aunt were located. He was directed to the gardens, where he hastened to without delay. The Bennets might have considered it rude, except that Mrs. Bennet was still much too excited by the return of Mr. Bingley.

"Nephew," Lady Catherine called out, walking in his direction. "I have come to resolve this situation."

"What situation are you referring to?" Darcy asked.

"Your ridiculous engagement to this woman!" Lady Catherine exclaimed, pointing her walking stick in the general direction of Elizabeth.

"Please be careful what you say," Darcy replied. "The only way that this 'situation' will be resolved is when Miss Elizabeth and I are married."

Darcy walked past Lady Catherine, to stand next to Elizabeth. He pulled her hand into his before he turned and faced his aunt again.

"Unless you have come to wish us well, I suggest you take your leave."

"I will not be talked to in this manner," Lady Catherine replied. "You will return with me at once. I have just finished explaining to Miss Bennet that we will have a retraction placed in the newspaper immediately. It will list her engagement to Mr. Lucas, and yours to Anne, explaining that there was a mix-up with the original announcement."

"You will desist, immediately!" Even Lady Catherine could not mistake the anger in Mr. Darcy's voice. "Now, for your sake, I hope you have not repeated this nonsense to anyone else, especially not the Lucas's."

It would seem today was not the day for Lady Catherine to win a staring contest. Finally, she replied.

"No, I have not yet made my intentions known to the Lucas family. I have plans to pay them a visit after leaving Longbourn."

"You will listen to me very carefully. You will return to your carriage and return home. You will not contact me or Miss Elizabeth again until you are ready to apologize and give us your best wishes. I will be marrying Miss Elizabeth, and there is nothing you can do to stop it."

With a huff, Lady Catherine returned to her carriage, making it to London before nightfall. The next day, instead of heading directly to Rosings Park, she decided to pay her brother a visit. She hoped that by bringing the Earl of Matlock to her cause she might have some success. She knew that Darcy had often turned to his Uncle for advice after his father had passed. In this endeavor, though, she was unsuccessful. After receiving the news of Darcy's engagement they had questioned Colonel Fitzwilliam concerning the young lady in question. He gave his parents such a glowing review of Miss Elizabeth that they were predisposed to approve of her. If anything, Lady Catherine's complaints served to strengthen their plans to welcome Elizabeth into the family with open arms.

In the end, Lady Catherine was compelled to return to Rosings Park in defeat. Her dissatisfaction extending to most in her presence, causing the Collins's to plan an extended visit to Charlotte's family. Fortunately, Lady Catherine had made no mention of her plans concerning Elizabeth and one of Charlotte's brothers, so they did not have that additional gossip to discuss.

"How are you, my dear?" Darcy asked, after watching Lady Catherine depart.

"How do you expect me to be?" she replied with a smile.

"I can only apologize for my aunt's horrible manners. It will not happen again. If you were any other young lady, I would expect you to be quaking in your boots, but you are Elizabeth Bennet. You are not intimidated by anything. I almost wish you were ready to fall apart so I would have an excuse to pull you into my arms to comfort you." Although he was trying desperately to appear as if he had his emotions in check, it was clear was greatly disturbed.

"Since when do you need an excuse to pull me into your arms," Elizabeth replied. "We are engaged."

As it turned out, Darcy was the one to receive the greater amount of comfort by pulling his beloved into his arms. Their comforting embrace was only to last a few minutes, as Mr. Bennet had sent

Mary to find them as soon as Lady Catherine's carriage was seen to leave. Chaperone back in place, Darcy and Elizabeth resorted back to holding hands while strolling through the garden, always within sight of Mary, who was peacefully sitting on a bench enjoying a book.

Chapter 11

Jane was greatly distressed. After Mr. Bingley arrived at Netherfield Park, Elizabeth had shown her the engagement announcement for the young lady to whom he had previously been engaged. Her emotions were all in an uproar. She was not ready to speak with him alone.

Elizabeth had promised Jane that she would not leave her alone with Mr. Bingley. Although she had been successful for a few weeks, the machinations of Mrs. Bennet could not be avoided forever. Georgiana had arrived, with plans to stay at Netherfield Park until the wedding, and she had gone to the dressmakers with Elizabeth for a fitting of her wedding gown. Mr. Bingley took this opportunity to visit Longbourn on his own. Within moments of his arrival, Jane found herself quite alone with him in the drawing room.

Trying her best to appear aloof, Jane sat quietly, stitching Elizabeth's new initials on some handkerchiefs.

"Miss Bennet, as we are alone, I would beg you to allow me to share my feelings with you," Mr. Bingley said.

"I do not think we will be alone for long," Jane replied. "Perhaps it would be best if you refrained from expressing yourself."

"I am afraid that my feelings are of a nature that I can remain silent no longer. I love you with all my heart. It was foolish of me to stay away for so long."

"You cannot mean what you say," Jane interrupted, quite distressed.

"But, I am quite sincere," he replied. "I should have overcome every obstacle that was before me and returned to your side as soon as I could. I am convinced there is no other woman who would make me a better wife.

"Not even Miss Crawford?" Jane asked quietly with her head bowed.

Bingley's face paled. When Darcy had admitted to him that he had concealed Jane's presence in London, he did not say anything about Jane being aware of his previous engagement. When Bingley did not immediately reply, Jane decided to ask the one question that had been burning in her mind since Bingley's arrival.

"If I was not aware of your previous engagement to Miss Crawford, would you have told me about it?" Jane asked.

Although the look of pain that crossed Bingley's face was answer enough, he attempted to explain himself.

"I did not see a reason to impart news that could only bring you pain, and that was now irrelevant. What I felt for Miss Crawford was a passing fancy. I cannot help but be glad that she has broken the engagement. What I feel for you runs so much deeper. It is a love like nothing I have ever felt before. I believe that you love me as well. Can you not understand that I would have asked you to marry me long ago if I was not already bound to another? Now that I am free, will you not consider marrying me?"

"I am sorry, Mr. Bingley," Jane replied. "It would be a lie if I were to say that I do not love you. Unfortunately, love is not enough. I find that I do not trust you, and a marriage where there is love but not trust would be misery."

"Please reconsider," Bingley begged. "I would do anything to prove my love for you."

"You do not need to prove your love," Jane replied. "You need to prove your faithfulness. You came to fall in love with me mere months after proposing to another woman. How can I trust that your heart would stay true?"

"I have loved you these many months that we have been apart," Bingley replied. "Is that not evidence of my faithfulness?"

"Please, we cannot continue this conversation," Jane replied, with tears in her eyes. "I have given you my answer, and I will not be swayed. Unless I can trust you with my heart, I cannot marry you. I am afraid that I have been in love with a dream."

"I will make it my ambition in life to prove my worth to you," Bingley replied.

Jane found that she could no longer keep her composure, and quickly excused herself from the room. Mrs. Bennet was standing in the hall, hoping to express her congratulations to the happy couple. She was not to be given that pleasure. Seeing her eldest (and most beautiful) daughter retreating to her room in tears, Mrs. Bennet was quite put-out with Mr. Bingley. Convinced that Jane was withdrawing in defeat, she decided to join Mr. Bingley in the drawing room to discuss Jane's many excellent qualities that would make her a most agreeable wife. She had barely spoken two words, though, before Bingley excused himself and returned to Netherfield Park.

Mr. Bingley had every intention of gaining Jane's trust, but first he had a friend to confront. There was only one person who could have told Jane about his engagement to Miss Crawford. Disappointed in Jane's refusal, he let his feelings of unhappiness find a new target. *If Darcy had not told Jane about Miss Crawford, then surely we would be engaged by now. What right did he have to share that information?*

Fitzwilliam Darcy was enjoying a rare moment of solitude. He loved Elizabeth very much, and had come to appreciate her family, but could not but look forward to the time that they would be appreciating them from afar. Georgiana's visit had brought some peace to his life, as he could not but approve of the growing friendship between his sister and his future wife.

This morning, Georgiana had accompanied Elizabeth to the dressmakers for a fitting of Elizabeth's wedding gown. It was evident to Darcy that Elizabeth was doing her best to include Georgiana in the wedding preparations, but since she had turned everything but the dress over to her mother, there was little Elizabeth could do to include her. Thus, they had ventured to the dressmakers on their own this morning. Georgiana was thrilled.

After sending Georgiana off in the carriage to pick up Elizabeth at Longbourn, Darcy had retreated to the library. He had not taken a moment of quiet reading and reflection since Bingley had arrive at Netherfield Park, especially as Georgiana arrived only a few days later. He had promised his sister and Elizabeth that he would join them for tea at Longbourn, but that was still several hours away.

When Bingley suddenly burst into the library, Darcy suddenly felt guilty for neglecting his host this morning. He was unaware that Bingley had also taken the opportunity provided by the expedition to the dressmakers to make an appearance at Longbourn, so the first words out of Bingley's mouth caught him completely unaware.

"What right had you to tell Miss Bennet of my engagement to Miss Crawford?" Bingley practically shouted in accusation.

Knowing that his friend was caught up in his emotions, Darcy took a deep breath before answering.

"I had not intended to discuss your engagement with Miss Bennet," Darcy replied.

"Then how did she come to know about it?" Bingley asked.

"She overheard a conversation between Miss Elizabeth and myself," Darcy replied. "I was not aware she had drawn close enough to overhear our conversation. I am sorry that her knowledge of your previous engagement has given you distress."

"Of course it has given me distress!" Bingley exclaimed. "She now says that she does not trust me enough to marry me. That marriage to me would be misery."

"Where those her words?" Darcy asked, confused. He could not imagine Miss Jane Bennet using such strong words.

"Yes, but if you had not informed her of my previous engagement she would have no reason to refuse me. I could be speaking to her father at this moment, instead of letting out my frustrations. What right did you have to share my engagement with anyone? Even if it was your precious Miss Elizabeth."

"I am sorry, but Miss Elizabeth was asking me about whether or not you would be returning to Netherfield Park. I finally confessed to her that I did not expect you to return until after your wedding. I meant it to be a private conversation, but Miss Bennet was closer than I realized. She did not mean to overhear, but could not hide the fact that she had."

"And why could you not have warned me that she knew?" Bingley asked. "If I had known she was aware of my engagement I would have discussed it with her before asking for her hand. Instead, as I was trying to ask for her hand she asked me about Miss Crawford."

"Do you mean to say that you had not intended on telling Miss Bennet about your previous engagement? What excuse would you have given for your extended absence?"

"If the subject came up, I had intended to tell her that I had been kept away by business and family concerns, she need not have known I had other reasons."

"You really would have started a life with the woman you love without an acceptable reason for being gone the better part of a year?"

"I love her, why should the rest of it matter?"

"Maybe, when you are able to answer that question, you will be able to ask for her hand again."

Darcy sincerely hoped that his last comment was true. He had often seen his friend fall in and out of love, but even he had to admit that the feeling seemed to run much deeper this time. Hopefully, Bingley would be able to prove himself to Miss Bennet without half as much pain in the process as Darcy had experienced after the first time he had proposed to Elizabeth.

Elizabeth Bennet enjoyed her excursion with Georgiana. It was rare that the two of them had time to themselves. Typically, if Georgiana was at hand, then so was Mr. Darcy. Although Elizabeth wanted to get to know her future sister better, she was selfish enough to admit that if Darcy was around, she spent a vast majority of her attention on him. It was pleasant to have a morning dedicated to getting to know Georgiana.

After visiting the dressmakers, Elizabeth and Georgiana had visited the confectionary, indulging in a sweet treat before making their way back to Longbourn. This had given the two young women a chance to get to know each other better, and both were pleased by the further friendship. Georgiana could not but be glad that her brother was marrying such a lively, joyful young woman.

When they arrived at Longbourn, it was clear that something had happened. Mrs. Bennet was muttering something about Mr. Bingley having visiting by himself, leaving Jane in tears. Elizabeth knew she would not get an intelligent answer from her mother, and it quickly became apparent that there were no other witnesses to Jane's tears. Apologizing to Georgiana for leaving her alone with her family, Elizabeth went in search of her sister. She found Jane in her room, quietly looking out the window.

"Oh Jane, whatever is the matter?" Elizabeth asked.

"Mr. Bingley asked me to marry him, and I refused him," Jane replied. "But please do not tell Mamma. I do not think I could bear her reprimands." Jane could not stop the tears from overflowing her eyes.

"My dear Jane, I am afraid this is my fault," Elizabeth replied. "If I had not taken the morning to spend time with Georgiana you would not have been left alone with Mr. Bingley. Will you ever forgive my selfishness?"

"You cannot blame yourself for this," Jane said. "I have tried to avoid him since he returned to Hertfordshire. I should have been more pointed in my avoidance."

"Do not blame yourself. You are much too dear and sweet," Elizabeth said, pulling Jane into her arms. "Now that you have refused him, how do you feel?"

"Absolutely miserable," Jane cried. The tears were flowing freely down her face now. "I am afraid that I still favor him above any gentleman of my acquaintance. I wish that I could have accepted him. I am just afraid that marrying him would have made me even more miserable in the future."

"To be more miserable than this would be misery indeed," Elizabeth replied. "Now, let me help you into bed then I will read to you while you rest. It has been far too long since we have spent time alone."

"But will not Mr. Darcy be joining us for tea? You do not want to miss seeing him do you?" Jane asked.

"In just a few short weeks I will be marrying Fitzwilliam and leaving Longbourn forever. I think he can spare me for one day. I will just send a note down to Georgiana letting her know that I am taking care of my dear sister. She will tell her brother for me."

"I will miss you when you are gone."

"Yes, and I will miss you as well. I do not know what I will do without my dear, sweet Jane to comfort me."

"I am sure that Mr. Darcy is anticipating the time that he will be able to fulfill the role of confidant in your life. You will not miss me."

"But what about when I need to speak about Fitzwilliam! It would hardly be seemly to talk about Fitzwilliam to himself. No, I will be forever looking forward to your visits. You must promise me that you will be a regular guest both in town and at Pemberley."

"I will be there anytime that you ask," Jane replied.

The two sisters continued their conversation, reminiscent of so many others that they shared while growing from youth into young ladies. Although Elizabeth never did end up reading to her, Jane did eventually fall asleep, fatigued from the emotional upheaval of the day. Elizabeth found an opportunity to return downstairs in time to wish Georgiana and Mr. Darcy a fond farewell, with a promise that they would spend more time on the morrow. As soon as the Darcy carriage was out of sight, Elizabeth ran back up the stairs to attend to Jane. Mrs. Bennet was preparing to lecture her on the need to spend as much time as possible with her intended so that he would not regret his decision, and Elizabeth would much rather not hear the dissertation.

Chapter 12

Charles Bingley tried to open his eyes, but the pounding in his head prevented him. Seeing his master stirring, Bingley's valet, Johnson, approached with powders and some water.

"If you will just sit up a little and take this you will feel much better soon," Johnson told him.

"Thank you," Bingley croaked out after taking the powders and lying back down. He was trying to remember why he would be in such pain. Then he remembered the empty bottle of port.

After Darcy left him to visit Longbourn on the previous afternoon, Bingley had decided to have a drink to calm himself down. The more he thought about the fact that Jane had rejected his offer of marriage, the more he drank. He had a dim memory of an empty bottle of port and a couple of footmen helping him to his room.

With a night's restless sleep, he came to realize that he had to apologize to his friend. He should not have been upset at Darcy because he had told Miss Elizabeth about his engagement to Georgiana Crawford. Since the engagement had not been announced before it was broken, he did not plan on telling anyone about it, even Jane. Although most of the world would have no reason to be told, he could not fault his friend for confiding in the woman he was going to marry.

With his new found determination to make amends with his friend, he slipped back into slumber, even though the sun had already risen in the sky.

Although Bingley had never been as early of a riser as Darcy, Darcy was still surprised that he had not yet seen his friend out of his room by the time he and Georgiana were preparing to leave for Longbourn. He contemplated (briefly) waiting for his friend to arise before leaving for the day, but he had only seen Elizabeth for a few moments the day before and was anxious to be on his way.

As the carriage pulled up to Longbourn he was transfixed by the vision of Elizabeth and Jane walking arm in arm through the gardens. When they heard the carriage, they turned their course to the entrance of Longbourn to greet their guests, though Jane seemed a little reluctant. When Darcy and Georgiana were the only ones to exit the carriage, Jane visibly relaxed. Clearly, she was not yet ready to face Mr. Bingley.

"Would you like to join us for a stroll before joining the rest of the family?" Elizabeth asked.

After receiving a positive glance from Georgiana, Darcy agreed to the proposal. They quickly repositioned themselves so that Jane and Georgiana were in front of Darcy and Elizabeth.

When Georgiana travelled to Hertfordshire to visit with her brother, Darcy had sent Mrs. Annesley on to London for a holiday so that she could visit with her children. Mrs. Annesley was scheduled to stay in London until the wedding, at which time she would travel to Hertfordshire. After the wedding, she would travel with Georgiana to Derbyshire so that they would be waiting for the newly married couple when they arrived.

Darcy and Elizabeth planned to go directly to the townhouse in London after the wedding. A week later, they would then travel to Pemberley. Even though they would be passing through Hertfordshire on their way, they were not planning on stopping.

While condoling with Jane the previous day, a plan had formed in Elizabeth's mind. It was clear that Jane needed a change of scenery.

"How would you feel about Jane joining us at Pemberley after the wedding?" Elizabeth asked. "She could easily travel with Georgiana and Mrs. Annesley."

"If you would like your sister to join us, she is more than welcome," Darcy replied. "Has she expressed an interest, or are you not ready to be parted?"

"Well, I wanted to talk to you about it before inviting her, but she would like to leave Longbourn for a short time. If we do not invite her to Pemberley, then I am sure that my Aunt and Uncle Gardiner would invite her to stay with them in London."

"Please, invite her to Pemberley. I am sure that Georgiana would be delighted with the extra companionship. It is always pleasant to have friends about."

The rest of the visit passed rather quickly. Darcy was surprised that Mr. Bennet chose to spend some time with the rest of the family instead of secluded in his library. He could not help but feel as if he was being observed (and he would be correct).

Mr. Bennet had given his consent to the marriage because he had seen evidence of the love that his daughter shared with Mr. Darcy. This did not change the fact that Mr. Bennet had to reevaluate everything that he thought he knew of the man. The conceited man that he thought he knew would never lower himself to track down the daughter of a country gentleman. Instead, he would break all ties with the family as quickly as possible, and encourage others to do the same. But that is not what Mr. Darcy had done. Mr. Darcy had saved the reputation of the Bennet family, then hid the fact from the very people that should be grateful to him. Mr. Bennet was coming to realize there were unseen depths to his future son-in-law. He still did not appreciate that Mr. Darcy was taking Elizabeth away from him with very little warning, but he could appreciate the fact that Mr. Darcy was a much better man than he initially thought him to be.

Mr. Bingley finally got the opportunity to apologize to his friend late that evening. He had spent much of his day (or what was remaining of his day after he arose around two in the afternoon) riding his horse around the countryside. The more he thought of his actions the day previous, the more he realized he needed to apologize to his friend. He still would have preferred that Jane had never learned of his engagement to Miss Crawford, but he could not fault Darcy for confiding in his betrothed. It was just unfortunate that Jane overheard. He was not yet ready to admit that he was at fault for not telling Jane of the broken engagement.

The two men were sharing a glass of port before retiring. After feeling so dreadful that morning, Bingley was only sipping a little at a time. He was not ready for a recurrence of the previous evening.

"I am sorry for the way I spoke to you yesterday," Bingley began.

"I know you were upset," Darcy replied. "Think no more on the manner in which you spoke to me. We have been friends for a long time. I know what it is like to be rejected."

"When have you ever been rejected?" Bingley replied with a laugh. "You should choose a different way to commiserate with me. I cannot imagine a lady that would reject you."

"You need not imagine her, you have met her," Darcy replied. "Elizabeth rejected me the first time that I asked. She leveled such accusations against me. I was so upset that I broke with all propriety and wrote her a letter. Although I had no hope that her affections could change to such an extent that she would agree to accept me, I could not live in the world with her believing so ill of me."

"How long did it take her to change her mind? Did she accept you after reading your letter?"

"I do not know how long it took. After I gave her my letter I walked out of her life, never expecting to see her again. She did not seek me out. I spent months thinking of her without any hope that she would return my sentiments. I have never been more pleased to see anyone as I was to see her touring Pemberley with her Aunt and Uncle Gardiner."

"And how long did it take you to come to an understanding when you met her again?" Bingley asked.

"We were engaged by the end of the day," Darcy replied, hoping that Bingley would not notice that his ears were turning red while thinking of that day.

"What do you think made the difference? Why did she accept you the second time?"

"The first time I was very condescending. I focused on how much she would gain through marriage to me, and degraded her family. By the second time I proposed I had come to appreciate everything about her, including her family. I was not as conceited as I had been. I had changed, and she noticed."

"Do you think that I have any hope of changing Jane's opinion of me? Do you think she will ever accept me?"

"I cannot answer that question," Darcy replied. "I do not know how to encourage someone to trust you. I know that she was hurt by your deceit. She has good reason to worry about the constancy of your heart. I do not know how you would venture to prove to her that you will remain constant. Time may be your greatest ally."

"But what if she finds someone else to love?" Bingley asked.

"Then you will need to let her go," Darcy replied quietly.

"I do not know if I can do that."

"You may not have a choice."

As the weeks marched slowly by marking the time until the wedding, Darcy came to appreciate Elizabeth more and more. At every dinner party they attended, he knew his heart would be lightened just by looking toward his Elizabeth. She would smile and his heart would be lighter.

This was especially true after Mr. and Mrs. Collins began their visit with Charlotte's family. Elizabeth was pleased to see her old friend, but knew that Darcy found the company of Mr. Collins to be tedious.

Throughout this time, Bingley did his best to blend into the background. He could not bring himself to leave Netherfield Park, as he did not want to be far from Jane, but Jane had made it clear that she did not currently desire his company.

Three days before the wedding, Netherfield Park received an influx of visitors. The first to arrive was Miss Bingley and Mr. and Mrs. Hurst. They were followed shortly by Colonel Fitzwilliam, his parents, and his elder brother. No one was surprised when Lady Catherine chose to decline her invitation.

The next day, Bingley hosted a dinner at Netherfield Park, providing an opportunity for Darcy's relations to become acquainted with the Bennets. Caroline Bingley would have been lying if she would have expressed a wish for the dinner to progress smoothly. Even though she had told herself several times that it was hopeless, there was still a small voice in the back of her head telling her she had one last chance for Mr. Darcy to recognize that she would be a much superior choice as his wife.

Sadly, Caroline's unspoken wish was to remain unfulfilled. She could hardly believe how welcoming the Earl of Matlock and his family were to Eliza Bennet and her family. She was even struck with the contrast to her first meeting with the Fitzwilliams. They had not been quite as welcoming. Even now, she got the distinct impression that they were being friendly to her out of politeness.

After dinner, one and all were gathered together in the drawing room, enjoying some entertainment before the Bennets left for the evening. While Mrs. Hurst played the pianoforte, Caroline sidled up to Mr. Darcy and Miss Elizabeth.

"I do not believe I have taken the opportunity to congratulate the two of you," Caroline said, with quite an insincere smile pasted to her face.

"Thank you, Miss Bingley," Elizabeth replied. "Your felicitations are most welcome."

"I am looking forward to the day that I can wish your dear sister happiness in marriage as well," Miss Bingley continued, addressing herself to Mr. Darcy.

"I appreciate your sentiments, though I can assure you that will be quite some time in the future. She is only sixteen," Darcy replied.

"Yes, but I am sure she will be one of those beautiful debutantes that finds herself engaged before her first season is even finished," Miss Bingley said. "I am sure we will all meet again at Pemberley this time next year to wish her and her chosen suitor well."

"Although I have no doubt that my sister will attract many suitors during her first season, I am afraid that we will not know about it by this time next year. Miss Darcy has asked to wait an extra year to be presented."

"That does not seem fair to the young gentleman that is waiting until the end of her first season to make his intentions known to the world," Caroline replied.

"I can assure you there is no such young gentleman," Darcy stated.

Caroline was confused. She knew that a year previous she had overheard her brother talking to Darcy about his engagement to Georgiana, and the need to wait until the end of her first season to make the engagement known. She did not know what had changed.

Scanning the room for her brother, she found him standing in a corner, with mournful eyes turned on Jane Bennet sitting with Colonel Fitzwilliam and his brother. *Had her brother foolishly broken his engagement with Georgiana in order to pursue Jane Bennet?*

It should be noted that Charles Bingley was completely unaware of the look on his face. He was also completely unaware that Caroline had overheard a part of his conversation with Darcy and had jumped to the conclusion that he was engaged to Georgiana Darcy, instead of Georgiana Crawford. So, when all the guests had left for the evening, he felt ambushed when Caroline came to his door and demanded a word with him.

"What has happened between you and Miss Darcy?" Caroline demanded immediately.

"I am not sure what you are talking about," Bingley replied, confused. Truth be told, he could not remember even talking to Miss Darcy that day.

"I am talking about the fact that you are no longer engaged to her, and instead you are mooning over Miss Bennet," Caroline stated.

"I was never engaged to Miss Darcy, where did you get that idea?" Bingley asked.

"A year ago, while in London, I heard you talking to Darcy. You were discussing the fact that you were engaged to Georgiana, but would wait until after her first season to make it known."

"You should be aware by now that when you overhear a conversation you do not always hear all the relevant details," Bingley replied. "We were not discussing Miss Darcy. I was engaged to a different Georgiana, but you need not worry trying to determine her identity as she has since broken off the engagement."

"Who was this woman? Why did she break off the engagement?" Caroline asked, trying to catalogue all the Georgianas she was acquainted with to determine the probability that her brother would have been engaged to them. She had to admit there were several Georgianas introduced into society recently, as so many families had decided to name their children after King George. There were at least five young ladies introduced just this year alone.

"You need not concern yourself with who she is. Her father broke off our engagement in preference for another suitor. She will be married very soon."

Miss Bingley, satisfied that she would be able to determine who her brother had been engaged to by determining all the Georgianas that were to marry soon, launched on to another subject.

"Well, then, why are you mooning over Miss Bennet?"

"I do not define glancing in her direction from time to time as 'mooning over her,'" Bingley replied.

"You were doing much more than glancing at her from time to time. You were positively staring. If you are not going to approach her, you should turn your gaze elsewhere. Just because you were not engaged to Miss Darcy does not mean you cannot cultivate a relationship with her. In a few years you could marry her, after all."

"Caroline, I have no desire to cultivate more than a brotherly relationship with Miss Darcy. Darcy and I have been friends for a very long time, but I do not think our friendship would survive if he were to find me trying to engage his sister's affections."

"And why not?"

"Because he knows that my feelings lie elsewhere."

"If you are determined not to pursue Miss Darcy, then why do you not just declare yourself to Miss Bennet and be done with it. With Mr. Darcy marrying Miss Elizabeth, you would then be brothers. We would always be welcome in his home."

"I thought you did not like Miss Bennet? Did you not encourage me to stay away from Hertfordshire?"

"Miss Jane Bennet is a sweet girl. No one could find any fault with her, even if she does come from an atrocious family. I encouraged you to stay away because I was under the impression that you were engaged. Even you should know it is not kind to trifle with a young lady's affections."

"I never had any intentions of trifling with her affections."

"Then why did you show her such marked attention when you first took possession of Netherfield Park?" Caroline asked. "The neighborhood was under the impression that you would be making an offer, but you were not free to do so."

"Would you please just let this be?" Bingley finally asked. "I am tired, it is time to retire for the evening."

As Caroline left her brother's rooms she started contemplating what steps to take next. It appeared as if her brother was set against a relationship with Miss Darcy. He was now free to court Miss Bennet, but also seemed disinclined to approach her. Although a year ago she would not have favored a match between her brother and Miss Bennet, the match would now also connect them to the Darcy name through marriage. That was a favorable outcome. Deciding that she needed to talk to Jane to push her in her brother's direction, Caroline settled down for the night. She was not unaware that the Fitzwilliam brothers had both spent much of the evening in Jane's company. She could not let this opportunity to become aligned to the Darcy name slip through her fingers. She may not have won Mr. Darcy's hand, but she still had hopes to have a connection between them to further herself in society.

Chapter 13

Elizabeth Bennet woke on the day of her wedding full of nervous anticipation, her head still reeling from the talk she had with her mother the night before. She squeezed her eyes closed, trying to banish the sight of her mother's giddy face as she explained the "secret pleasures" that could be found in the marriage bed. Although the talk had given her some reassurance for her wedding night (especially after Charlotte's advice to "close your eyes and breathe deeply and it would soon be over"), she found that she would have rather her mother had never talked to her at all.

Elizabeth quickly dressed in her morning dress, and descended the stairs for breakfast before readying herself for the wedding. When she came upon her father enjoying his breakfast, she found she could not look upon him without blushing, and hastily retreated to her room. She did not know how she could ever look either of her parents in the eyes ever again. There were some things that children really did not want to know about their parents.

Elizabeth could not remember a time that she had ever seen her mother and her three remaining unmarried sisters work so well together. They all did their best to help her prepare for the day. For their part, they all had very different thoughts running through their heads.

Kitty was already composing her letter to Lydia in her mind. She was still perturbed at all the trouble she had gotten in when Lydia had eloped, and was planning on describing every detail of the elaborate wedding in excruciating detail. She knew that Lydia's wedding was a very quiet event.

Mary was daydreaming about finding a man such as Mr. Darcy to marry. She had never given much thought to the romantic side of matrimony, but seeing the way that Mr. Darcy and Elizabeth showed their affection for each other, she came to realize that she wanted that for herself. She still had very strict ideas about morality and the purpose behind marriage, but admitted to herself that it would be much more pleasant if she found a man that would love her. She had dried the roses he had gathered for her in the garden with Elizabeth. They were now some of her most prized possessions.

Jane was excited for her sister, but was also trying to hide a bit of melancholy. She would not disturb her sister's special day with her disappointment. She had been trying to forget about Mr. Bingley, so had done her best to give her attention to the Fitzwilliam brothers, but she was always painfully aware of his presence in the room. She could not wait until the next day when she would travel with Georgiana and Mrs. Annesley to Pemberley. She was sure that if he was not always in her presence she could forget about him, now that she knew he had been engaged when he had gained her heart.

Mrs. Bennet was occupied imagining all the things that her daughter would be able to buy with her pin money. If her daughters heard her occasionally sigh the words "ten thousand a year" they chose to ignore it.

It was time. Elizabeth found herself standing outside the chapel doors with her father, waiting for the music to change to announce their entrance. Elizabeth was grateful that her father had eventually supported her marriage to Fitzwilliam Darcy, but she was sad that their relationship would likely never be what it once was.

"Lizzy," Mr. Bennet said quietly, "I want to tell you how sorry I am for causing you pain. I should have listened to you when you told me that you had fallen in love. I thought you were just trying to spare my feelings. Once I opened my eyes, it became obvious that you care for Mr. Darcy very much."

"Papa," Elizabeth replied, "I should not have lost my composure when you first told me you planned to refuse your consent. If I had not run away crying, perhaps I would have been able to convince you of my love for him."

"I am just glad that you will be happy. It would have been painful to part with you to anyone less worthy."

"Thank you, Papa," Elizabeth said, with tears in her eyes. "I have missed you these last few months."

Just then the music changed, announcing it was time for them to make their entrance.

As Mr. Bennet escorted his favorite daughter down the aisle, all eyes were turned to the blushing bride. At first Darcy was concerned when he saw the evidence of fresh tears on her face, but the glorious smile she sent in his direction allayed his fears. He had never seen a more beautiful sight.

Elizabeth knew that her sister Jane was at the front of the chapel, ready to stand up for her. She also knew that Colonel Fitzwilliam was at Darcy's side. She was also cognizant of the fact that the chapel was filled with well-wishers. She was aware of all these things, but she did not see them. She only had eyes for Darcy.

The wedding went by in a blur. Somehow the happy couple were able to say all the right things at the right time. They signed the register, then were making their way back down the aisle, with Jane and Colonel Fitzwilliam trailing behind.

The wedding breakfast went by in a blur for Mr. and Mrs. Fitzwilliam Darcy. As soon as possible, they found themselves saying goodbye to their friends and family, and climbing in the carriage to take them to London.

The wedding breakfast was torturously long for Miss Jane Bennet. She was seated next to Colonel Richard Fitzwilliam. She enjoyed his lively wit, and was doing her best to keep up her end of the conversation, but every time Bingley came into view her words would falter.

"I cannot help but notice your distraction, Miss Bennet," Richard said. "If you would prefer, I will relinquish my place for Mr. Bingley."

"That will not be necessary," Jane replied, with a panicked look in her eyes. "I would rather not talk to that gentleman at the moment."

A look of concern washed over Richard's face. Miss Bennet was now his cousin by marriage. With Darcy away with his enchanting new wife, he decided to determine if there was anything that he needed to talk to Mr. Bingley about. It would not be right if Mrs. Darcy's sister felt uncomfortable around any of her husband's friends.

"Is there anything you would like to tell me, Miss Bennet? I know I am not your new brother, but Darcy and I have always been close, especially after the death of his father when we were left as joint guardians over Georgiana. If Mr. Bingley makes you uncomfortable I will talk to him."

"No, please do not do that," Jane replied, blushing profusely. "It is nothing that time will not resolve."

"Are you certain? If Mr. Bingley has done something to make you uncomfortable, I would like to be able to help you in some way." Richard was a little confused. Although not a close friend with Bingley, he had always assumed he was a good sort of fellow. He did not know what Bingley could have done to disconcert Miss Bennet.

"I am certain. Mr. Bingley has proven his ability to quickly recover from disappointment. And, now that I know the inconstancy of his heart, I will recover as well."

"Has Mr. Bingley had some sort of disappointment? I was unaware."

"Most would consider a broken engagement to be a disappointment."

Richard was shocked speechless for a moment.

"Do you mean to tell me that Bingley was engaged?" he asked. Although untitled, and a background in trade, Bingley was wealthy enough that he was considered a reasonably good catch. It amazed him that he was unaware of Bingley's engagement (or the much more scandalous fact that it has been broken).

"Yes, he was engaged before coming to Netherfield Park last year. He did not make it known, and proceeded to show a preference for my company. I came to prefer his company above that of others, when he disappeared back to London without a word. When the engagement was broken he came back. Without an explanation about his engagement, he proceeded to propose. I did not feel I could trust him with my heart."

"If you do not mind me asking, how did you discover his engagement?" Richard asked. "I have not heard even a whisper about him being engaged, or the inevitable scandal that would result from a broken engagement. Is it possible you were mistaken?"

"I overheard Mr. Darcy telling Elizabeth about it. After Mr. Bingley proposed, I asked him about it. His only defense was that he did not think I would ever know about it, so did not think it would matter."

"Although I cannot begin to understand how that would have made you feel, I can tell you that no one was aware that Mr. Bingley was engaged. It is very likely that you never would have heard a word about it if you had not overheard Darcy talking to your sister."

"That may be true, but that does not make it right. I can only hope that my future husband would always want to be honest with me. Starting out by omitting a very important aspect of his recent life does not reflect well on his ability to be completely open and honest with his wife."

The conversation soon moved to more trivial matters. Before long, the younger Miss Bennets came to claim Jane to wish the newlyweds goodbye.

As everyone waved goodbye to Mr. and Mrs. Darcy, Caroline Bingley saw her chance for a private tête-à-tête with Jane Bennet, as well as to steer her away from rejoining Colonel Fitzwilliam, who was now engaged in a lively discussion with his brother and Miss Darcy.

"Jane, dear, how lovely to see you again," Caroline exclaimed with a false smile firmly plastered on her face.

Jane could not forget the way that Caroline had treated her in London, and tried to extricate herself as quickly as possible.

"Yes, it has been quite some time since your last visit to Gracechurch street," she replied. There was a slight twitch in Caroline's eye at the mention of Gracechurch Street, but she had determined her course, and would not be swayed.

"You must be so lonely with your dear sister gone away," Caroline continued. "I was just talking to Louisa about how pleasant it would be for you to join us at Netherfield for a few weeks. Perhaps you could even return with us to town for the Little Season."

"I am sorry, Miss Bingley," Jane replied (not feeling sorry at all), "but I have been invited to spend the next several weeks at Pemberley. I am leaving with Georgiana in the morning."

Silently fuming that she had not been invited as well, Caroline continued her flattery, to no avail. Eventually, Jane was able to make her excuses and leave Caroline's side. Not wanting to face anyone else, she slipped through the hedgerows into the wilderness to the side of Longbourn.

Charles Bingley had been watching Jane Bennet from the moment she walked into the church that morning. He could not but feel remorse for the fact that if he had behaved differently, he could be looking forward to his own wedding with the beautiful angel. Watching her converse easily with Colonel Fitzwilliam since his arrival sent sharper pains into his heart than he thought possible.

Charles completely understood why Darcy had asked his cousin to stand up for him instead of himself. Not only had the two boys been as close as brothers since their youth, but Darcy did not want to make his new sister uncomfortable. Darcy was aware of the strain that currently existed between Jane and Charles. Charles had been his friend for many years, but Jane was his new sister.

As he watched Jane slip between the hedgerows, he decided he would try to talk to her one last time before she left for Pemberley in the morning.

"Good day, Miss Bennet," he said after finding her sitting on a secluded bench.

Jane jumped at the sound of his voice. Glancing at him, she gave him a small nod in greeting before looking back down. It was obvious she had been crying. The sight of tears did him in.

Quickly falling to his knees, he pulled out his handkerchief and offered it to her.

"Please do not cry, Miss Bennet. Is there anything that I can bring to bring you relief? A glass of wine perhaps?"

"No, there is nothing wrong. It has just been an emotional day." She quickly looked away, though she did take his handkerchief, using it to dab at her eyes.

After a few minutes of silence, Mr. Bingley formed a resolution. Things could not possibly get much worse between him and his angel. He might as well try to explain himself.

"Miss Bennet, may I begin by apologizing for my behavior toward you," he said. "I should have told you about my engagement to Miss Crawford the moment I realized I was developing feelings for you. I convinced myself that I could have you as a friend. After the Netherfield Ball I realized that my feelings were of such a nature that friendship was not a real possibility. I left for London the next day to break off my engagement. Before I could do so, I was reminded that my honor was engaged. It would be wrong to break off the engagement. I allowed myself to be convinced that you did not really care for me. Instead of returning, I took the coward's way out. I remained in London."

He paused in his story, taking the opportunity to stand and pace. Jane's face was a complete mask. When she simply took a deep breath, looked away, and asked him to continue, he started talking again.

"The months after leaving here were horrible. I felt guilty for loving a woman who was not my betrothed. I rarely visited Miss Crawford, certain that she would be able to tell that my heart was otherwise engaged. Balls and dinner parties lost their appeal because I knew you would not be there.

"I cannot describe to you the joy I felt when Miss Crawford broke our engagement. Her father had asked that it remain private until the end of her first season. Darcy was the only person outside of her family that was even aware of the engagement. I know that does not excuse my behavior. I should have told you why I did not immediately return and ask for your hand. I know I made a mistake, and can only hope that I can prove myself to you in some way."

When Bingley was done with his explanation, they remained quietly in each other's company for a couple of minutes. When Bingley was ready to give up on a response and return to the others, Jane finally spoke.

"How long were you privately engaged to Miss Crawford?"

"It was close to year," Bingley replied, surprised at her response.

"I am not yet ready to form an attachment to you," Jane stated. "I must admit that even with your explanation I fear allowing you to possess my heart." When her voice broke on the last word, Bingley was close to coming undone.

"Please, what can I do to prove how ardently I admire and love you?"

"I think that all we need is time," Jane replied, sadly. "If your feelings remain true for a year, then you can celebrate the Darcy's first anniversary by paying a call at my home. If your feelings have not remained true, then do not pay that call. I will understand."

"Thank you for giving me this chance, Miss Bennet. I will not fail you."

Elizabeth had never felt happier. As soon as the carriage was away from Longbourn, Darcy closed the shades then proceeded to express himself as sensibly and as warmly as a man violently in love can be supposed to do.

After all the trials they had faced, they were finally married. And alone. By themselves. With no witnesses. Nothing could be better.

After what felt like a matter of moments, the young couple was exiting the carriage at Darcy house in London. The staff exchanged knowing glances as the master made the introductions then scooped up his new wife and carried her to her chambers, claiming they were quite fatigued and would retire for the evening, even though it was only four in the afternoon. They were only rarely seen over the next week, preferring to take their meals in their rooms.

As the Darcy's prepared to travel to Pemberley, he promised that on their next trip to town he would make sure Elizabeth was better acquainted with the rest of the house.

Epilogue

Jane and Georgiana enjoyed their time at Pemberley getting to know each other before Darcy and Elizabeth joined them.

Jane stayed with the Darcys for the better part of the year. Her friendship continued to grow with Georgiana, and they soon found they had much they could discuss (including embarrassing stories of their respective siblings).

Caroline Bingley never did determine which Georgiana her brother had been engaged to, as there were three young ladies by that name that were married within weeks of each other. After finally being forced to give up her determined pursuit of Mr. Darcy, her eyes were opened to the impoverished nobility. It was not long before she had used her dowry to buy herself a husband, and a title. Unfortunately, the family was impoverished for a reason. It was not long before her husband had gambled away her dowry, and they were left in poverty once more, only being recognized in society because of their title. Even that was taken away when her husband was killed in a duel, leaving his younger brother to assume the title. Bitter at the world, she took her place in the dowager house, along with her mother-in-law. No longer having a dowry to recommend her, she became little more than a paid companion to her late husband's mother.

Lydia Wickham never could fully forgive her sister for marrying so soon after she did, and to a man of such greater wealth that her wedding was hardly even mentioned. This did not stop her from pressing her sister for monetary help at every given opportunity.

Kitty Bennet also spent much of her time at Pemberley, though she could not claim the same level of intimacy with Georgiana as her sister Jane. It was not long before the influence of her elder sisters helped her become much more reserved when in company, though she was still a little wild when alone. She was caught climbing a tree by a Captain in the Navy as he was passing through to visit family in Derbyshire. She refused to give him her name, convinced he would leave soon and never remember her. Unfortunately (or fortunately) for her, his family was acquainted with the Darcys and their entire party had been invited to a dinner party to welcome home their younger son. They were married before he had to return to the sea. Kitty found that she preferred the blue coats of the Navy over the red coats of the Army.

Mary Bennet was the only Bennet daughter to stay in Hertfordshire. She had never been blind to the discord in her home, but had always assumed most marriages were similar. She had learned from her sister's example that there was another way. She was obliged to mix more with the world, and as she was no longer mortified by comparisons between her sisters' beauty and her own, it was not a sacrifice. She soon found that she preferred the company of John Lucas above that of any others, and they were wed with very little fuss. They first time he gathered roses for her by himself she cried with such delight, and rewarded him so ardently, that it became a regular habit.

In order to give Mr. Bingley the chance to visit at her home on the Darcy's anniversary, Jane ensured she was at Longbourn on the long awaited day. Even though Mr. Bingley was suffering from an unseasonal bout of pneumonia he showed up at their door at the crack of dawn, practically passing out in the entranceway. Jane had been both dreading and anticipating this day, not knowing if Mr. Bingley would pay his visit. When Mrs. Bennet found her eldest daughter practically laying on top of a man in their entryway the shrieks could be heard for miles around. Since Mr. Bingley was nearly unconscious the action could hardly be blamed on him, though he gladly agreed to be married to Jane as soon as possible.

Colonel Fitzwilliam married his cousin Anne, and resigned his commission. After taking her away from her mother's influence he was able to find a doctor that was able to recommend treatments that actually helped. Although never particularly robust, she was able to bear a son and a daughter before they decided it would be best if they did not try again. Richard's elder brother, Andrew, was killed in a hunting accident, leaving Richard as the next Earl of Matlock. Anne mused that her mother should be happy that two of the Fitzwilliam estates had been joined in marriage, just not the two she had planned.

Elizabeth could never have the relationship with her father that she once had, but his apology went a long way toward healing the breach. Eventually, he was welcomed to Pemberley, and he delighted to visit, especially when he was least expected.

When Fitzwilliam Darcy had come across Elizabeth Bennet touring Pemberley and embraced her, no one could have imagined that they were starting a tradition. To the continual embarrassment of their nine children, anytime Fitzwilliam was called away from home, he would be greeted on his return by his wife with a passionate embrace, no matter their location on the grounds. The servants soon grew accustomed to the displays of affection that often resulted in Mrs. Darcy being carried to her chambers for a short respite from the day. Their eldest son swore he would never forgive them for embarrassing him in front of his friends from university who were visiting on one such occasion. Although their eldest daughter had also been mortified, she soon learned to forgive her parents when she married one of her brother's friends from Cambridge and they started a similar tradition.

The End

Made in the USA
Middletown, DE
19 November 2015